Sid slam rb. 'Are you feeling a

Sid turns he windscre ar first. He curses so ge your attitude.

'Vasecto

'Facetiousness has got to stop. If you're going out on the shop floor you've got to do so in the right attitude. Serious, alert, responsible —'

'Hang on a minute,' I say. 'Shop floor? I thought you were taking over this place?'

'And you thought you were going to end up with some cushy number sitting behind a big desk?' Sid shakes his head. 'Oh no, Timmo. It's not going to be like that. That's the besetting sun of British industry, that is. Management up there, workers down there. With me at the helm, it's going to be different . . . I'm not condemning you to the shop floor. I just feel you should have the opportunity to come to grips with industry at all its levels . . . This way . . . there can be no complaints . . . It's democracy in action.'

Also by Timothy Lea in the Confessions series

CONFESSIONS FROM THE POP SCENE
CONFESSIONS FROM A HEALTH FARM

Timothy Lea

Confessions from the Shop Floor

Futura Publications Limited

A Futura Book

First published in Great Britain in 1974
by Futura Publications Limited

ISBN 0 8600 7147 2
Printed by Oxley Printing Group Ltd.

Futura Publications Limited
49 Poland Street
London W1A 2LG

CONFESSIONS FROM THE SHOP FLOOR

Chapter One

In which brother-in-law, Sid, considers a business venture and Timmy takes dusky Pearl home to meet Mum and Dad — unexpectedly.

Chapter Two

In which Timmy and Sid visit The Universal International Bed Centre — later Slumbernog — have trouble effecting entrance, meet Managing Director, Jeremy Rightberk, and Shop Steward of the S.C.A.B.s (Sedan Chair and Bedmakers) Fred Umbrage, and in which Timmy shares a gastronomic and rather sordid experience with some tubs of cream and two excitable ladies.

Chapter Three

In which Timmy joins the work force of Slumbernog and experiences the strange ritual of 'Nut Squidging' in the Stuffing Department. Also in which he attends a union meeting and is introduced to the mysteries of the Cuddle Chamber — a bed-testing centre.

Chapter Four

In which Timmy attends a Board Meeting at the A.C.D.C. ('Artisan Controllers' Dining Club) and meets Plantagenet, Maitland, Henry and Crispin Rightberk. Also, some topless waitresses who perform unusual services for their customers below tablecloth level.

Chapter Five

In which Timmy helps deliver a bed to man-hungry Mrs Collier and hovers on the periphery of an orgy of extravagant sexuality and violence.

Chapter Six

In which Timmy works alongside Professor Nuttibarm in the Development Centre and even more closely alongside the Professor's assistant, Jean, in the Cuddle Chamber — a period of flat-out effort that has an explosive climax.

Chapter Seven

In which a pleasant idyll at the Lea home is interrupted by Chief Inspector McGoolygrab and in which Timmy learns some startling news about Professor Nuttibarm and HM Government's interest in beds. Also in which Timmy is tempted — and succumbs

Chapter Eight

In which the S.C.A.B. trip to Tolpuddle heads for Southend and a good time is had by all — except the parents of the bride and one or two stockbrokers.

Chapter Nine

In which Timmy shares an unexpected pleasure with his managing director's wife — and is disturbed.

Chapter Ten

In which Slumbernog hovers on the brink of a serious industrial dispute and Comrade Nitya Pullova arrives from the USSR to make a considerable difference.

Chapter Eleven

In which Sid entertains Timmy and pushes the boat out in a big way.

CHAPTER ONE

In which brother-in-law, Sid, considers a business venture and Timmy takes dusky Pearl home to meet Mum and Dad — unexpectedly.

'I've answered this advertisement in *The Times,*" says Sid.

'*The Times*?" A note of surprise enters my voice. My brother-in-law is not exactly what you might call a typical *Times* reader. He tends to find *Exchange and Mart* a bit highbrow.

'Oh yes, Timmo. It's a very good paper. Excellent foreign section, very sound on the arts — and it takes 10p worth of chips, no trouble.'

I might have guessed. Sid does all his reading off the magazines Mum cuts up to put in the toilet, or what he finds down at the doctor's when he is trying to get a medical certificate.

'So what was it about, Sid?'

'Some geezer wanting capital to extend a profitable business venture.' Sid takes a reflective sip at his pint and my blood runs cold. Sid's business brain works with the remorseless speed of a glue glacier and his eye for a good thing is matched only by a rabbit trying to have it away with a bacon slicer. He reads my expression. 'It can't do any harm to have a look, can it? I mean, if it's in *The Times* it must be all right.'

'It doesn't mean it's all right,' I say. 'It just means it doesn't read dirty. They don't check everything.'

Frankly, I am amazed that Sid still has any money left. I believe he did all right out of the insurance when Beauty Manor burned down — you read all about that in *Confessions from a Health Farm,* didn't you? — but he doesn't talk about it a lot. Frankly, I am not surprised. Sid's relationship with Sir Henry Baulkit and Wanda Zonker was confusing and probably very unhealthy and I think that when Wanda disappeared Sir Henry was only too glad to lash out a hefty slice of the insurance money to keep Sid's mouth shut.

'What does this bloke do?' I say.

'He makes beds,' says Sid.

'Domestic help?' I say. 'You don't want to get mixed up in that, Sid. You'll end up with water on the knee. That's women's work.'

'Manufacturing beds, you berk!' rasps Sid. 'Not farting about with hospital corners. Gordon Bennett! Can you see me as a housemaid?'

'Roll your trousers up and I'll tell you.'

'Get stuffed!' Sid knocks back his drink and shoves the glass towards me agressively. 'It's your turn to get them in. I'm not made of money, you know.'

'Everybody knows that,' I tell him. 'They call you Mr Abstinence because you never go for a p.'

'Piss off!' Sid always descends to coarseness in the face of superior word power and I take our glasses to the bar and wonder what harebrained scheme he can be considering. The more half-witted it is, the more likelihood there is of Sid parting with some mazuma. I remember Hulapog — the game where you hurled surplus pogo sticks through unwanted hula hoops. He sold four sets. Still, beds doesn't sound too outlandish. Lots of my best friends have beds. I have passed many a happy hour on them myself. Many people actually sleep on them. Could it be that Sid has actually found a product with a future? I am not sorry to be getting the beers in because — apart from the fact that I am one of nature's givers — they have a new bird behind the bar who is quite an eyeful. She is of the tinted variety and though not as dark hued as Matilda Ngobla — whose dusky loins I once decorated — she is considerably browner than most brands of toothpaste. She has a lovely pair of top bollocks — slung like cannon balls waiting to be bunged into the breach — and a dark red mouth that makes me think of the texture of rose petals — you can tell I haven't had my end away for a couple of weeks, can't you?

'What is your pleasure?' she says.

This is the kind of question that can get a few funny answers even though the Highwayman does cater for a nicer class of person these days. Because I think I might get a bit further with a sophisticated approach I resist the easy descent into roguish raillerie and suggest that the consumption of another couple of pints from the wood might go some way towards satisfying my desires.

'Not many people about,' I say, gazing down the front of her dress as if I expect to find a pair of feet sticking out from between her knockers.

'It's always quiet on a Monday.'

'I haven't seen you in here before, have I?'

'I don't know. I'm not your eyes.' While I think about that, she pushes the pints towards me with short jabs of her fingers and gazes into my minces. 'I help out sometimes when Gladys wants a night off. We probably haven't overlapped.' She smiles when she says it like the word 'overlapped' means to her what it means to me. '32p, please.'

'And a packet of crisps,' I say, applying slight pressure to the palm of her mit as I slide the ackers across. Talk about gentle love play. This is more like the Calmer Sutra than the Kama Sutra.

'What flavour appeals to you?'

'Just stick your hand in the tin and see what you come up with.' She smiles at me and bends over to plunder the cartons of goodies. She has a beautiful bum and a classical case of V.P.L. (Visible Pant Line) showing through her jeans. I go a bundle on that. Any glimpse of underwear always gets percy trying to prize the lid off the counter.

'Cheese and onion all right?'

'Favourite. Ta, luv.'

'That'll be another 4p, please.'

'Do you fancy anything yourself?'

She flashes her lashes at me. 'Not just now, thanks.

'See you later, then.'

I return to Sid and slop a gobful of pigs over the table in front of him. 'Blimey, you're a clumsy sod, aren't you?' he says pleasantly. 'I never met anyone so bleeding useless when it comes to carrying things.'

It occurs to me to comment that I have been carrying my brother-in-law for years but I restrain myself. Sid's idea of a heated discussion is trying to shove his fist inside your earhole.

'Sorry, Sid. I'll get a cloth,' I say.

'Don't bother. Your handkerchief will do.' He snatches it out of my pocket and starts mopping up the beer. 'It's in a disgusting condition,' he says. 'Did you use it for doing an oil change?'

'My handkerchief? No, I dusted your chair with it.'

Sid leaps to his feet and rubs his german over his here and there like he is trying to touch it up. He is wearing his posh new trousers and is very sensitive.

'Taking the piss, as usual,' he says sitting down again and chucking my snitch rag in my lap. 'You're a right little bundle of fun, aren't you?'

I don't answer because there is no point and the bird behind the bar is giving me the glad eye. Why should one man have so much? It doesn't seem fair really.

'Nice bit of stuff, that,' says Sid.

'Who? What?' I say.

'Don't play dumb with me! The brown tart. Gordon Bennett! I thought you were going to announce your engagement when you were getting the beers in.'

'Dad would like that,' I say.

'What, the bird or the engagement?'

'Both. You know what he's like with those Ngoblas. It's horrible what goes on in that mind. All that prejudice wrapped up in steaming lust.'

'Terrible,' agrees Sid. 'Your Mum's the same isn't she? She was always terrified that the Ngoblas would start spreading. Do you remember when she thought she heard something in the attic? She thought they were coming through from next door and living there.'

'Eventually taking over every attic in the street. Yeah, I remember. The chair fell over and she was left hanging, wasn't she? It gave her lovely long arms, though.'

'Fred Nadger has had her,' says Sid.

'Not Mum!' I am horrified. I know we live in permissive times and Fred certainly puts it round a bit but —

'Not your mother! The tart behind the bar. Gawd help us! Can you imagine anyone having a go at your mum?'

When I think about it — which I don't like doing — I can't. Not even Dad. Not for years, anyway. The red blood flowing through his veins dried up to a trickle before I could tell the difference between him and Mum.

'Don't be coarse, Sid,' I say. I greet the news about Fred Nadger with mixed feelings. I am glad to hear that the bird does a turn but I am not over enthusiastic about following in Fred's footsteps — or whatever. I never like to think of other blokes spoiling something beautiful that should be reserved entirely for Timothy.

'He said she was a right little raver,' says Sid. 'She comes from Trinidad. You know, in the West Indies. I reckon they're all a bit on the jungle bunny side out there. Start rattling your tom toms and the old breasts are thundering up and down against the chests so that you could hammer rivets with them.'

'Delightful,' I say. 'Is Fred all right? Not walking about like an upright concertina?'

'He looked all right when I saw him,' says Sid. 'In the pink, or you might say, in—'

'Yes,' I say, heading off Sid's salty wit before it gets to the pass. 'I know what you mean.'

Sid takes a long swig from his glass and wipes the back of his hand with his mouth. 'You know, I like the idea of making things.' I look at Miss Trinidad polishing a glass and nod. 'I'd like to play my part in putting this old country of ours back on its feet.'

'Back on its back, don't you mean?' I say. 'I mean, beds and all that.'

'Don't make feeble jokes. I'm serious. Money isn't everything, you know.'

'Are you all right, Sid?' I sniff my pint suspiciously. There must be something in it — there is plenty of room because it isn't overloaded with hops.

'It's this money-grabbing philosophy which is at the root of most of our national ills. Everybody out for number one and devil take the hindmost.' I can hardly believe my bottles. If Sid helped an old lady across the road she would probably find that she had lost her handbag before they were half way over. Sid must see the expression of incredulity on my mug. 'Of course, I know that I've erred in the past. I've been as guilty as anybody when it came to looking after number one. I've been overbearing, dictatorial—'

'Oh no, Sid,' I interrupt. 'You haven't. You've been —'

'Shut up when I'm talking!!' snaps Sid. 'What was I saying? Oh yes. I made the mistake of thinking that money was the only thing that mattered. I forgot about the importance of job satisfaction. What's the point of having a lot of bread if you're miserable?'

'What's the point of being miserable if you've got a lot of bread?' I say.

Sid thinks for a minute. 'Yeah, well, that's one way of looking at it, too. But believe me, Timmo. It doesn't work like that in practice.'

'I've never had the chance to find out,' I say.

Sid clears his throat. 'That's where you've been lucky.. I'm glad I've been able to spare you that. It can be very disillusioning.'

'Thanks, Sid.' I now realise why Sid took all the cash from our previous exploits and never paid me anything. He was protecting me from disappointment. What consideration, what humanity, what a load of bleeding rubbish!!

'I want to put what I've learned to some use,' says Sid plaintively.

The bird behind the bar is standing on a stool to reach down a carton and I nod enthusiastically. 'Very creditable,' I say.

'We've worked on both sides of the fence in our time,' drones Sid. 'We know the problems. If we can harness management and labour to a common purpose — a purpose not just connected to financial reward — then we can start moving forward again. We can give the whole country a lead. Noggett Beds will set an example to British Industry.'

'You're leaping ahead a bit, aren't you?' I say. 'You haven't even talked to the bloke yet.'

'That's my mandate,' says Sid. 'You don't get anywhere these days unless you've got a mandate.'

'I thought a mandate was something you gave to someone else,' I say.

'You can give yourself one if you want to,' says Sid. 'It's still a free country — more or less.'

I am pretty certain that neither of us knows what a mandate is so I don't press the point. The point I would like to press is the blunt job between my legs. Where I would like to press it depends on the trowel behind the bar although I can see one or two likely spots without having to consult Gray's Anatomy.' ('Trowel' equals a small spade.)

'Don't rush into anything. That's all I ask you,' I say. 'If that bloke has to advertise to raise cash there must be something wrong with him. Why won't the banks lend him the money?'

'He probably doesn't want to pay all that interest. I expect he's offering a better deal. A stake in the company.' I doubt if Sid would get a stake in the company if they were manufacturing palings but I don't say anything.

'Well watch it. There's a lot of mean people about.'

'I've met some of them,' says Sid. 'The kind of blokes who wouldn't crash the crisps if they were having tea at Buckingham Palace. Mean, self-seeking people —'

'All right, all right!' I say, dropping the packet in his lap. 'You have these. I'll get some more.'

I skip to the bar and Miss Trinidad lilts across, shaking her bum like a sulky moggy. 'What do you want, man?' she says.

'Another packet of crisps, please.'

'Any flavour you have in mind?'

'The ones you have to bend furthest for.' I wink at her just to show that I'm joking and it is all good clean fun — well, fun, anyway.

'Saucy.' She bends down kicking one leg up behind her and fishes out a packet of crisps between finger and thumb. 'Plain,' she says, glancing at the packet.

'They don't remind me of you.'

'Flattery will get you anywhere,' she says. She is right of course. Be it ever so horrible there is no substitute to laying it on with a shovel. Women do respect sincerity and if you say they look beautiful then they automatically think that you must be sincere.

'You pack up at closing time, do you?' I ask, lowering my voice. I can see the guvnor looking at me suspiciously and I don't want any trouble. I have been told not to come back more times than our next door neighbour's tom.

'When we've tidied up,' she says.

'We might go on somewhere?' My voice becomes husky and enticing — at least, it tries to.

'Like where?' I was afraid she would ask that question. The smarter birds usually do. I was thinking of behind the changing rooms where they store the goal posts but I wanted it to be a surprise — it was certainly a surprise the last time I was there. I had just got this bird pressed up against something solid when all the crossbars fell down and buried her knickers. Very lucky she wasn't wearing them at the time. It put the kibosh on our romance though. I stepped back a bit sharpish and sat in one of the washing troughs — my trousers were round my ankles, you see. It wouldn't have mattered but some sloppy bastard hadn't bothered to take the plug out. Talk about a passion killer. It wasn't all that warm to start off with.

'I could take you home,' I say.

'What, to your place?' This had not been my intention but the hint of interest in her voice makes me think again. Mum and Dad usually go out less often than the tide in the Mediterranean but some mate of Dad's at the lost property office — where Dad works and furnishes our home — has got him involved in a rotarian's ladies night. Of course, Dad didn't want to go but Mum nagged him rigid. She said the last time Dad took her out was to see 'Brief Encounter' — they didn't get in because there was a queue — and thirty years later she feels like hitting the high spots again. Dad groans and moans about the cost of the tickets — especially when he finds that the cost of what he thought was a double is for a single and that wine is not included — but Mum gets her way in the end. 'Don't worry about the wine,' she says wittily. 'I've had enough whining from you to last me a lifetime.'

I seem to recall that the tickets said 'Carriages 2 am' — Dad thought it meant real carriages, stupid old git — so my esteemed parents should be out of the way long enough for me to cement a meaningful relationship and be snug in my cot by the time they lumber through the front door.

'Yes,' I say. 'Come back for a drink.'

'Oh,' she says. 'That will make a change.' I think she is trying to be sarcastic but I don't take her up on it.

'I can run you home afterwards,' I say. That is literally correct. Provided I am still capable of running I will be quite willing to lope beside the young lady as she leaves the purlieus of Scraggs Lane, from time immemorial and immortal the home of the Leas. If she is expecting a car she will be disappointed.

'All right,' she says. 'But I won't be able to stay long.' I have to suppress a smile. They all say that. It is like Turkeys making plans to visit the in-laws on Boxing Day.

'How did you get on?' says Sid when I sit down again.

'Salt and vinegar,' I say. 'Do you fancy one?'

'Don't treat me like I'm soft in the head,' says Sid. 'You were trying to get that bird to go out with you, weren't you?'

'I was just being pleasant,' I say. It never pays to tell too much to Sid. Although he is married to my vivacious sister, Rosie, he is not above thrusting his pelvic area and appurtenances into close contact with any lady's mole-catcher. He has seen more crumpet than your friendly local baker — in fact it was Sid who gave the trade the idea of putting holes in the middle of dough nuts — and he does not mind playing with his friends' toys.

'Going to take her home, are you?'

'I was thinking about it,' I say. 'But there are nine of them in the flat. You know what it's like? Her mum's just come back from Nightingale Lane with another one.'

'You find a lot of them down there,' says Sid. 'Ah well, sup up. No sense in being downcast about it. Women aren't everything, are they?'

'You're right, Sid,' I say, trying to sound as if I am putting a brave face on it. 'There's comradeship, isn't there?'

'A few pints of ale between friends. What could be better. Drink up, Tim lad. You don't fancy a short, do you?'

I have never known Sid so full of the milk of human kindness. It is practically curdling in the face of the unexpected warmth. As I stand in the gents wondering why anyone should want to write 'I had my sister in a pair of wellington boots' on the pebble dash wall — I mean, it is so difficult apart from anything else — I also chew over whether Sid is preparing himself for the key role he intends to play in the bedding business — I must say it does seem the right business for Sid.

I later learn that my naive faith in Sid's good nature was misplaced. I have just helped Pearl — yes, that's her name — remove something rather unpleasant from her shoe — those platform jobs don't half spread it around — and the lights at the edge of the common are in sight when she starts moaning. 'I'd have taken your friend's offer if I'd known,' she says. 'Do you want your handkerchief back?'

'You must be joking,' I say. 'What offer?'

'He said he'd take me up west for a meal.' Sid only meant West Clapham but it is still a better offer than I came up with. The crafty sod! No wonder he was keen to get up to the bar.

You can't trust anyone can you?

'He's got a Rover 2000, hasn't he?'

I decide to ignore this remark. 'Lovely night, isn't it?' I say. 'I do like a stroll.'

I don't mind a stroll. It's hiking I object to. You told me it was just round the corner.'

'Once we get off the common it's just round the corner.' She is not exactly overdoing the pre-foreplay, this one. I hope I am not dooming myself to disappointment. It is distressing how white hot favourites can sometimes turn colder than last year's Christmas pudding. There is no accounting for women.

'Cut across here,' I say. 'Sorry mate.' I am addressing the uppermost of the two people I have just tripped over. It is so dark once you get off the path. The bloke makes a strange grunting noise but I don't think he is talking to me.

'Disgusting!' says Pearl. 'Why did you have to bring me this way?'

'It's a short cut,' I say, trying to steer her away from the bloke who is throwing up in the waste paper basket. 'If we go — no.' I don't think that couple against the tree are studying lichen. Knickers! It is not exactly the best introduction to a night of wild passionate ecstasy. Most of these people seem to know each other rather better than we do.

By the time we get to 17 Scraggs Lane I am humming to keep my spirits up.

'Is this it?' says Pearl. She sounds as excited as some bird being fixed up with Frankenstein's monster on a blind date. I know they don't live in rude mud huts in Trinidad — polite mud huts at the worst of times — but I was not expecting to be taken to task for the family home.

'These houses are very sought after in Putney,' I say, quoting something that Mum is always saying.

'It must have heard,' says Pearl. 'It's leaning towards Putney.'

'Very funny,' I say, opening the front door and sticking my tongue out at Mrs Tanner our new neighbour. She is always peering through her lace curtains and it drives me round the twist. Once I took Dad's moose head round and tapped it against her front window and she had a police car on the door step in two and a half minutes flat. I had only just closed the back door behind me when I heard it screaming down the street. I wish I could have caught an earful of what she told them. They didn't hang about for long. 'Now, tell me, madam. Was there anything particularly distinctive about this moose? Anything you would remember if you saw him again?'

'No officer. I'm afraid he was just like any other common or garden moose.'

'It makes it very difficult for us, madam. Are you absolutely certain he had no distinctive features? Listen. I'm going to read you a list of things he might have been wearing in order to jog your memory: surgical truss, bowler hat, long pants — over the trousers. MCC blazer.'

'Why are all these gas masks hanging in the hall?' says Pearl. She sounds slightly frightened and very unimpressed.

'My father collects things like that,' I say. 'He's fascinated by anything to do with war.'

Pearl shudders. 'Sounds unhealthy to me. What about the wooden legs?'

'They came from North Staffordshire. We use them as firewood.' That doesn't sound very nice, does it? I wish Dad would nick a more superior class of article from the lost property office. It is difficult to explain the situation to visitors. They would never believe some of the things people leave on trains. Dad is like one of those Scavenger Beetles that goes around disposing of lumps of shit. He gets rid of the stuff that nobody claims. Society owes him a debt really.

'Does the barometer wo-'

'Don't-' Too late. The glass has fallen off again. People will keep tapping it. 'It's waiting to be mended. You didn't see which way the hand went did you?'

It is difficult to see anything in the hall because after the cost of electricity went up again our wattage came down to a level which would cause complaints at a teenagers' snogging party. You can hardly see your hand in front of somebody else's tit. It does create rather a gloomy atmosphere and I can see that Pearl is having no difficulty in resisting the temptation to shout 'Fiesta!' and run round the front room with one of the plastic roses between her teeth.

'Come into the drawing room,' I say. I call it the drawing room because of some of the things my nephew Jason Noggett drew on the wall with his felt pencil — I don't know where a child that age hears the words, really I don't. Unfortunately they didn't come off without smudging and this meant that the settee had to be moved against the wall to hide them. This liberated a large stain in the middle of the carpet and a pink latex brassiere which nobody claimed, neither of them. Sid said that Dad must have brought the bra home from the L.P.O. which didn't go down very well. In order to cover the stain. Mum moved the fireside rug but this revealed all the scorch marks and holes where I had tried to pick out the pattern of the carpet with a red hot poker — of course, I was just a child at the time and I didn't really know what I was doing — until the fire brigade arrived, that is. In the end, Dad solved the problem by bringing back a screen which we were able to put against the wall where Jason had done his stuff — I mean, the writing. At first, I thought the screen came from the L.P.O. but when I read that a bloke had fallen down a manhole on to some geezers who were repairing a power cable, I had another think. The initials L.E.B. were a bit of a give away, too.

'There we are,' I say proudly. 'Do you want to watch telly while I get us a cup of tea?'

'Have you got a colour set?' she asks.

'Oh yes,' I say. 'What colour would you like?'

'What do you mean?' She sounds startled. Maybe I should have explained. It isn't exactly a colour set. It's a black and white set and Dad got hold of these strips of tinted perspex. You prop them in front of the screen to get a colour effect. It is not very realistic and the perspex is so thick it is difficult to see the picture. Still, it is quite ingenious, isn't it? Unfortunately, Pearl does not seem to agree with me when I explain it to her and starts poking around the room — not a bad idea when you come to think of it. 'What are the dentures doing at the bottom of the fish tank?' she says.

The correct answer must be, 'growing a kind of green mould', but I do not give it. 'They must be Dad's,' I say. 'Jason — he's my little nephew — was messing about with them. Dad will be pleased.' At least, he will be pleased that they have been found. It is not surprising that nobody has noticed them up to now. The tank is pretty dirty and the dentures look not unlike an ornament as they sit grinning amongst the coloured gravel.

'Don't get them out now,' says Pearl with a shudder as I start rolling up my sleeve.

'All right,' I say. I can see what she means. The sight of Dad's best gnashers covered in green slime doesn't exactly make you come out in a romantic flush. 'Tea or coffee?'

'What kind of coffee is it?'

'Nescafe.'

'Do you have any real coffee?'

'It is real coffee. Out of a jar.' I suppose coming from Trinidad she doesn't know about things like that.

'I'll have tea thank you.'

I don't argue with her but flash into the kitchen. It is now getting on for midnight and I don't have a lot of time to waste. Dad should soon be taking Mum in his arms for the last mazurka. I clean the dribbles off the teapot spout with a rag I find in the sink and start bunging things on a tray. Some uncouth bugger has helped himself to the sugar with a wet teaspoon so there are unattractive brown lumps and streaks all through the basin. I get cracking with rag and fingers and try and clean things up. In the end I find it easier to bury everything under a fresh avalanche of sugar. The kettle is taking a long time to boil which I find is because I have switched on the wrong ring. Dear oh dear. I hope it isn't going to be one of those nights. I try and put a gloss on everything by digging out some cakes I find at the back of the cupboard but it occurs to me that the little chocolate flakes may be mouse droppings so I abandon the idea. The yellow icing was going a nasty transparent colour anyway, as I find out when I try and scrape away the mould. Blimey, this bird had better turn up trumps after all the effort I am putting in. In the end, I settle for some soggy biscuits and lug the whole lot back on a tray.

'I'm afraid we're out of milk,' I say.

She looks at me in a funny sort of way. 'You needn't have bothered,' she says. 'I can't drink it without milk. Is this what you brought me all the way here for, a cup of black tea?'

I put the tray on top of the telly and sit down beside her on the settee. A straight question deserves a straight answer. 'No,' I say. I gaze into her minces and suck in my breath sharply as if her wild animal beauty defies description.

'What is it?' she says. 'Has one of my lashes smudged?'

'They're perfect,' I say. 'Like-like-' once again she can feel me struggling for words '-like you. You're just too much.'

'Do you feel all right?' she says.

'I know it sounds ridiculous me talking like this,' I say. 'But I can't help it. It's the effect you have on me. You draw the words out of me — words I never thought I could utter. It's some strange kind of magic.'

'Do you have a proper drink?' she says. 'Something alcoholic. The way you go on I should think you must have.'

I cannot help feeling that I am not getting through to her. The old verbal magnetism is dropping a bit short of target.

'I'll have a look,' I say. 'I know we were running low'. Understatement of the year. Last Christmas we must have been the only family in the land toasting the Queen in Stone's Ginger Wine. Ever since I was a kiddy I have looked at a bottle of scotch like it was inside a glass case. I open the lower door of the sideboard and glance inside. There are a number of cork table mats which have been attacked by mice, a paper streamer and a pile of yellowing Christmas cards going back to the early fifties. Mum says she keeps the cards because she likes the pictures but it is really because it is the only way we can get a mantlepiece-full. When we get a Christmas card it is like another family getting a present. Everybody gathers round and it is passed from hand to hand and turned over to see how much it cost and if it came from the 2p section at Woolworths. The best card we had last year was addressed to somebody else and came to us by mistake. First of all we opened it to look at it and then we kept it. It showed a lot of geezers in top hats blowing trumpets from the back of a coach drawn by six black horses which are approaching an inn called 'Ye Swanne' practically buried in a snow drift. Inside, it said 'May all your Christmases be white, and future prospects mighty bright. Thinking of you this happy Yuletide, Harry, Doris and family — not forgetting Cuddles'. We thought about them a lot, especially Cuddles. I wonder what he was — or she, maybe. It was funny how the infrequent visitors to the house all picked up the card and nodded like they had known Harry and Doris all their lives. I hope we get something from them next year.

'Oh dear,' I say. 'That's amazing. You have to come at the one time when we're out of everything. Isn't there something else I can get you? We've got some cocoa.'

'I like cocoa without milk even less than tea without milk,' says my dusky dreamboat sulkily.

'Anything good on the telly?' I say. 'I see you've got it going.'

'Just an old movie,' she says. 'I don't know where they dig them up from.'

'It's probably black and white anyway,' I say, trying to cheer her up.

'Ronald Coleman,' she says. 'I can't see what anyone ever saw in him. That moustache.'

'The bird's all right,' I say, sliding on to the settee again. 'Her clothes look quite modern, don't they?' I advance my hand along the back of the settee and let my fingers brush against her shoulders. Neither of us is getting any younger and my brooding, passionate nature demands an outlet.

'Uum.' She doesn't tell me to piss off so I move my sensuous lips to her shell-like lobes and blow gently. She flicks her head like a disturbed cat. 'Don't do that.'

'How long have you been over here?' I ask.

'Eighteen years.'

'Eighteen years!' The scent of bougainvillea blossom is obviously long dead in this bird's nostrils.

'I came over when I was a baby.' She stifles a yawn. 'Have you got a record player or anything?'

'It's at the menders,' I say. In fact we do have a gramophone but it looks like the picture on an old HMV sleeve and was 'rescued' by Dad. I can't see Pearl's sophisticated tastes responding to it. Especially the selection of old Maurice Chevalier records that came with it. 'Lets make love,' I say. I suppose I could have built up to it a bit more but there is not a lot of time to waste and I need to know where I stand. It is also a fact that birds can sometimes respond well to the frank, straightforward approach. After all, they all know what it's about and they must get bored waiting for you to wring out the words.

'You don't wast a lot of time, do you?' she says.

'When you feel the way I do, there's not a lot of point.' I say. It doesn't mean anything but I put a lot of sincerity into it.

'Nobody could accuse you of trying to buy me, could they?' she says.

'I couldn't do it,' I say. 'I'm no saint but I do have a few scruples.'

This is another effective ploy. Just as birds are always prepared to believe you when you say something nice about them, they are also prepared to give you the benefit of the doubt when you say something nasty about number one. This way, you come out as being honest, in need of help, and slightly exciting. You can appeal to a number of their cravings with one simple approach. Frank Sinatra was a master of this gambit as a study of some of his old movies on the telly will reveal: 'If you know what's good for you, you'll stay away from me, kid. I'm poison to dames. I just foul them up, see? Stick with me and you'll earn yourself a groin-full of groans.' Of course, once he'd said that, knocked back a couple of fingers of Jack Daniels and flipped his snap-brimmed hat on to the back of his head they had to plane the birds off him in layers.

'It's not very romantic down here.'

Note the use of words carefully. She does not say 'in' here but 'down' here. This clearly indicates that the possibility of being 'up' somewhere has clearly entered her mind — as indeed it has entered mine. In her case I think she is thinking about 'upstairs'.

'Let me show you round,' I say, very casual. 'There'll be a collection for the National Trust at the end of the tour. Please give generously.' I run my fingers up her body as I get to the last bit and turn the telly off with a flourish. When she has helped me pick up the tea things we go out into the hall. I wish I was not so clumsy. Still, maybe she will put it down to my impetuosity.

'Where's the bathroom?' she says.

'Top of the stairs. Follow your nose.' She looks at me a bit old fashioned. 'I mean straight on.' I suppose I could have chosen my words better.

I take the tray into the kitchen and then I think of something. 'Watch out for the —' There is a shrill scream from the bathroom —' gorilla in the bathroom,' I finish lamely.

Dad keeps his gorilla skin in the bathroom because of the steam and it can give you a nasty turn if you're not expecting it — which, let's face it — very few people are.

'Oh my God!' says Pearl when I get to her side. 'I saw it in the mirror. I thought it was coming to get me.' The skin is hanging on the door and I can see what she means. Grab a gander at your mug and there it is leering over your shoulder.

'It's all right. I'm here,' I say, taking her in my arms and pressing my cakehole against her barnet. Well done, Dad's gorilla! This is just the little ice-breaker I needed. As I have said on many occasions it is vital to establish unforced bodily contact at the first opportunity.

'It's horrible!' she shudders I think she is referring to the gorilla but it may be the pressure of my giggle stick against her dilly pot that is causing anxiety. Percy is coming on strong as they say. Nothing feeds his base appetites more than the sight of a damsel in distress.

'Let's get out of here,' I say. I don't wait for her to consult her horoscope but lead her towards my room. A glance through the door makes me change my mind. I had forgotten that I had been stripping down the gear change on my bike. There are bits and pieces all over the bed. I don't want to sweep her on to it impulsively and find that I have wedged an axle nut up her khyber.

'In here.' I don't like using Mum and Dad's bedroom but passion makes you reckless, doesn't it? My high-thigh equipment is itching for action and in situations like this it is inclined to programme my thought box.

'It's all right in here, is it?' I see Pearl's eyes nervously scanning the walls for signs of gorillas or worse.

'You bet.' I take her cheeks between my hands and home on to her mouth like a bird settling on its nest. My tongue starts painting a mural on the roof of her mouth and I rub my chest backwards and forwards across her bristols. She is wearing one of those stretch silk blouses with puff sleeves and I flick my digits across the strawberries that show through. 'You've got a mole down there, haven't you?' I murmer. I am talking about her cleavage but she looks down at the floor as if imagining that the gorilla might have a friend. 'Here,' I say, sticking a finger down the front of her blouse.

'Yes. I never had it when I was a kid.' I don't make any comment but push her back on to the bed and start moulding the front of her jeans. I do wish birds would give up wearing trousers. I feel unhealthy touching up somebody turned out like a bloke. Mum's bed has an eiderdown on it and Pearl sinks into it so deep that you wouldn't be able to see her from the other side of the room. Not that I am going to look, mind you. I like it too much where I am.

I unpop the front of her jeans and then carry on popping up to the top of her blouse. She must have shapely knockers because they don't disappear when she is lying on her back. You know what some birds are like when in the Egyptian PT position — only their nipples mark the spots. I start fiddling for the catch on her bra but she shakes her head.

'It doesn't have one.' Funny how birds clobber changes, isn't it? I can remember when bra cups were like plastic beakers. Now they are as flimsy as Ted Heath's re-election prospects. I expose a couple of gnawable nipples and set to with a will — and a willy as I am reminded by the eager force battering the front of my brushed denim. You might well think that the back of my zip was a xylophone and that my love portion was practising its scales. My lips spill a confetti of kisses down to Pearl's tummy button and from this position I direct the assault on her jeans. Not that it is much of an assault. Pearl obligingly raises her shapely haunches and together we push the encumbering threads down to ankle level. She is wearing a pair of flowery panties and the white background sets off her light brown skin a treat.

'What about you.' Yes, what about me, indeed. With Pearl's unneeded help I rip open my shirt and wriggle out of my jeans like there is a prize for doing it fast. Percy bounds forward eagerly and only the frail fragment of my navy blue, silk-effect athlete's briefs keeps him in half-hearted check. Gently at first, as if tip-toeing across a minefield, Pearl brushes her fingers over my truncheon meat. 'He's keen, isn't he?' she says.

'Keen?' I say. 'He's a raving maniac!'

As I say this, her fingers take a steely grip on my hampton and she kisses me like she is trying to organise a tongue transplant. She may have been eighteen years out of the country but a lot of the old jungle magic still remains.

'Put him to work.' She arches her back and shows me her teeth — by opening her mouth, I hasten to add. She doesn't fish them out of her back pocket.

I am not the man to deny a lady such a request and I swiftly scramble to my knees and tug down her nicks. Her own fingers are not idle. She flicks down the rim of my pants so that Percy peeps over the top like we are having a punch and judy show.

'Peek a-boo!' she says.

Percy does not say anything. With him, actions speak louder than words as I hope to show the Caribbean curve carnival. Keeping my fingers in reggae rhythm, I check that all parts are in good working order and enthusiastic about the imminent arrival of Mad Mick. As she looks up at me expectantly I discard my pants and position myself on the starting grid.

'Go on.' That counts as the chequered flag as far as I am concerned. With a screech of balls I roar up the straight and head for the first bend. The Grand Prick of Clapham is under way. I could give you all the sordid details but I know that you are a sensitive bunch and would probably skip to the end of the chapter. Suffice to say that this chick performs like a mechanical sludge sifter gone berserk. I have never known such a mover. The bedhead bashes against the wall and the light in the middle of the room starts swinging. What a pity that one of us has to catch a toe in the eiderdown. That's right. Suddenly, the room is full of feathers. You have never seen anything like it. Talk about plucking a chicken. I feel more as if I am — what was that? I stop moving and my blood freezes. It sounded like the front door.

'I'd never have bleeding gone if I'd known he wasn't going to give us a lift back.'

'Oh, stop your moaning!'

Mum and Dad are back! Eek! Immediately, panic replaces passion, and my nunga wilts like a blob of fat at the bottom of a hot frying pan. My feet hit the floor and I start pulling on my jeans. Bugger! They are not my jeans. Bleeding unisex! Bleeding Sex!!

'Get your clothes on!' I hiss. 'They're coming!'

'I should be so lucky,' says the bird sulkily.

'I don't care about you. I'm going to bed.' That is Mum coming up the stairs. Oh my gawd! Why did I ever get myself in this situation? I must stop her coming in to the bedroom.

I brush some of the feathers off my shirt and hobble to

the door trying to wriggle my feet into my slip-ons. I fling the door open just as Mum's hand is stretching out for the knob.

'Timmy! What on-' I close the door behind me and stand in front of it.

'Did you have a nice time?' I say. A feather that has become attached to my lips soars into the air as I speak.

Mum stares at it suspiciously for a second before ignoring my considerate question. 'What were you doing in there?' she says. 'Why are you covered in feathers?'

She tries to go into the room but I continue to bar the way. Dad appears at the top of the stairs. He takes one look at me and stops dead. 'Blimey!'

They both stare at me and panic lights flash before my eyes. What can I say?

'Have you got someone in there?' says Mum. Dad grits his teeth and takes a menacing step towards me.

'You mustn't go in!' I squeak.

'And why not, pray?' snarls Dad.

'She's getting herself ready to meet you, 'I gulp.

'Who is?' Mum's voice rises sharply and she steps forward beside Dad.

'My fiancée,' I say.

'What!!?' They say the word together and take a step backwards like I have produced a gun. It is a masterstroke. Now they look bewildered. Seconds before they looked like a lynching party.

'Hi dere!' Pearl comes out of the bedroom smoothing the ruckles out of the front of her blouse at skirt level.

Dad catches Mum just before she hits the floor.

CHAPTER TWO

In which Timmy and Sid visit The Universal International Bed Centre — later Slumbernog — have trouble effecting entrance, meet Managing Director, Jeremy Rightberk, and Shop Steward of the S.C.A.B.s (Sedan Chair and Bedmakers) Fred Umbrage, and in which Timmy shares a gastronomic and rather sordid experience with some tubs of cream and two excitable ladies.

One of the strangest things about my "engagement" to Pearl is that Mum never mentions it — apart from saying that she will drop dead if we ever walk up the aisle together. She doesn't even say anything about the eiderdown. As a gambit — which is what I believe they call them in some circles — it is well worth remembering. The next time your mum or dad catch you on the job with someone, say that you're going to marry them. They'll be so horrified they won't bother to castigate you — it's OK, it doesn't mean what it sounds like. Sometimes I think that parents experience the reverse of what I feel when I imagine them on the job. It turns them right off to think of their little boy or girl indulging in all those nasty goings-on.

Of course, the fact that Pearl has joined the brownies without having to buy a uniform slips down less than a treat but it isn't the whole story. Sid hears about it from Rosie when she drops in to see Mum and he is full of interest as we drive to see Slumbernog — that is the daft name he has come up with for the company we haven't even seen yet. He was going to call it Slumnog until I spelt it out to him.

'You jammy old bastard,' he says. 'What was it like then? I hear they're a bit special.'

'Sidney, please!' I reproach him. 'Do you think I'm the kind who scatters the secrets of the nuptial couch?'

'But you aren't going to nupt her, are you?' asks Sid. 'I believe the ceremony is very embarrassing. You have to give her one while you're signing the register.'

'I don't know about that,' I say.

'All your relations standing about watching you,' muses Sid. 'I wouldn't fancy it.'

'Well, don't disturb yourself,' I tell him. 'It's not going to happen.'

In fact, nobody need get their knickers in a twist because I haven't seen Pearl since the night in question. I think she was a bit upset by some of the remarks Dad made. When he saw all the feathers in the bedroom he thought we had killed a chicken.

'Coming round here with your voodo love rights!' he kept shouting. 'We don't want no jungle loving in this house!' It was all very embarrassing.

'How much further have we got to go?' I say, deciding that the time has come to steer the conversation into less controversial waters.

'Just along here by the river. Nice, isn't it?'

I don't answer immediately because I am not certain whether he is joking. It depends whether you call boarded up buildings and collapsing warehouses nice.

'It seems to be coming down faster than a snail's knickers,' I say warily.

'That's good isn't it?' says my idiot brother in law cheerfully. 'Rents will be low and we'll be able to keep the overheads down.' He starts whistling "Old Father Thames" and rubbing his hands together.

'I should think the overheads will all be at floor level anyway,' I say. Sid slams on the brakes and pulls into the kerb.

'Are you feeling all right?' I say.

Sid turns off the engine and bashes his nut on the windscreen because he hasn't taken it out of gear first. He curses softly and faces me. 'You've got to change your attitude. All this fas-fash-vas —'

'Vasectomy?' I prompt.

'Facetiousness has got to stop. If you're going out on the shop floor you've got to do so in the right attitude. Serious, alert, responsible —'

'Hang on a minute,' I say. 'Shop floor? I thought you were taking over this place?'

'And you thought you were going to end up with some cushy number sitting behind a big desk?' Sid shakes his head. 'Oh no, Timmo. It's not going to be like that. That's the besetting sun of British industry, that is. Management up there, workers down there. With me at the helm, it's going to be different.'

'You mean it's going to be Sid up there, Timothy down there?'

Sid bashes his mit on the dashboard. 'There you go again. You can't be serious, can you? What I'm saying is that we've got to integrate ourselves with the labour force. We're all working to the same end. We've got to understand their problems, feel their grievances. And you can only do that by working alongside them.'

It has not escaped my attention that the "we" has changed to "you" at a very crucial moment. 'Are you going to work on the shop floor, too, Sid?'

'Up here,' says Sid. 'Up here.' A fanciable bird is passing the car and for a moment I think he is saying "Up her!" Then I see that he is tapping his nut. 'In my mind I will always be shoulder to shoulder with the workers. Their struggle will be my struggle, their sweat will be my sweat —'

'Their money will be your money. Come off it, Sid. Who do you think you're kidding? Why don't you go on the shop floor and I'll do what you're going to do?'

'Experience, Timmo. That's all it is. I've been forced into a role. You remember the position I held at Funfrall Enterprises?'

'It was on page forty-three of the Perfumed Garden,

wasn't it?'

'Management, Timmo. That's my forte. We've all got to do what we're best suited for. I'm not condemning you to the shop floor. I just feel that you should have the opportunity to come to grips with industry at all its levels, to work your way up through the organisational structure. Think of the effect it would have if the two of us came into the company and went straight to the top? You would understand dissatisfaction running rife, wouldn't you? This way, with you going in right at the bottom, there can be no complaints, can there? It's democracy in action."

'Uum.' I don't say anything because I can't really think of anything to say. I could dive out of the window but Sid has started the car again.

'Just think of it,' he raves. 'The Queen's Award to Industry.' Sid is wearing his light blue, collarless, two piece, slim fit and I think that he has got a better chance of receiving 'The Industry's Award to Queens'. Still, I don't say anything. Sid is always at his most sensitive when on the brink of a great enterprise — or cock-up as we in the business call them. I try to comfort myself with the thought that nothing is settled yet and that he may not go through with the deal but when I look in his gleaming eyes I have a nasty feeling that he is already choosing his office furniture.

'Here we are. Universal International Bedding Company. Henceforth to be known as Slumnog.'

'Slumbernog,' I remind him. 'Slums are broken down, disgusting places where no decent person would—' My voice trails away as I look through the padlocked gates into the squalid courtyard littered with rubbish and beyond to the crumbling buildings. 'I don't know Sid. Maybe it is quite a good name.'

'It slips off the tongue a sight quicker than Slumbernog,' says Sid. 'Now, I wonder how we get in?'

'There's a sign on the gates,' I say. 'It says "For admittance call opposite".'

We bend our eyes across the street and there is a broken down boozer called the Workers United.

'Looks more like Manchester United,' I say. 'Blimey. They can't mean that, can they?'

'Better have a look,' says Sid.

We park the car, decline the offer made by a couple of kids who want 50p to stop anybody removing the hub caps, fail to do business on the basis of them paying us 50p to avoid a clip round the carhole, and go into the pub. It looks like nobody has bothered to clean up since the Wako kid last hit town and has had no difficulty in resisting the temptation to tart itself up into the muzac and moquette bracket.

'Can you tell us how to get into U.I.B. mate?' says Sid to the ferret-faced geezer behind the bar.

'You looking for work?' says the bloke suspiciously.

At the word 'work', one of the old men who is playing dominoes in the far corner makes a high pitched squawking noise, clutches his throat and collapses across the table.

His partner stands up aghast. 'It's his heart,' he cries. 'Quick! Brandy.' With remarkable speed for a man of advanced age he rushes across the room and snatches the bottle proferred by the alarmed barman. Tearing out the cork he proceeds to drink greedily.

'What about him?' says Sid, indicating the gulper's stricken friend.

'Give him half a chance and he'll drink the lot,' says the man. 'Worst thing for him.'

'Give us a glass,' says Sid. He fills half a tumbler from the man's bottle and then proceeds to knock it back. 'That's better. I can't stand seeing people suffering. It makes me feel quite ill.'

'He should never have mentioned that word,' says the

man nodding at the barman.

'You mean work?' says Sid.

'Aaargh!' Immediately, the old man's head falls back amongst the dominoes and he slowly slides under the table.

'Now look what you've done!' The old man's friend springs to his comrade's side and proceeds to go through his pockets.

'Has he got some pills?' says Sid.

'Of course he has. Though he doesn't have much cause to use them, these days. What a damn stupid question. Ah, here we are.' The man removes a bulging wallet and places it in the inside pocket of his jacket. 'That should relieve the pressure a bit.' He takes another gulp of brandy and then, almost as an afterthought applies the bottle to his friend's lips.

'Are either of you anything to do with the factory?' asks Sid.

'I'm the gatekeeper and he's my mate.'

'What are you doing in here, then?' I ask.

'Keeping an eye on the gate, of course. Lovely view from here.' We follow his eyes through the pub window and it has to be agreed that by looking over the frosted glass it is possible to see the gate.

'You're a bit old to still be on the books, aren't you?' says Sid.

'Semi-retired, Fred and me,' says the man. 'But we like to do our bit for the old firm. I've been here man and idiot for nearly sixty years now.'

'And it don't seem a drop too much,' croons his friend who has made such a determined assault on the brandy that there is now only a couple of inches left at the bottom of the bottle.

'Can you let us in please,' says Sid. 'We have an appointment with Mr Rightberk at twelve.'

'I can't leave Fred,' says the man. 'Look he's finished that brandy and he still isn't moving.'

'Well, give us the key and we'll let ourselves in.'

'I couldn't do that.' The man sucks in his breath sharply. 'Oh no. I couldn't do that. Mr Umbrage wouldn't be holding with that, oh dear me no.'

'Who is Mr Umbrage?' asks Sid patiently.

'He's our shop steward. He's very hot on demarcation is Mr Umbrage. You so much as lay a hand on that key and the whole factory will be out.'

'All right, all right,' says Sid. 'We'll stay with your mate and you can go and open the gate.'

Fred's mate shakes his head.'Can't do that. It's a two-man job. One opening, one looking. If I open it and somebody belts out and does themselves an injury then I'm up the spout aren't I?'

'One of us can look.'

'You're not even on the pay roll!' The man's voice rises sharply. 'Are you an agent provocative, or something?'

'I'm just trying to get into the factory,' says Sid. 'I don't want to cause any trouble.'

'In that case, you'd better sit down and bide your time. Nobody is going in and out of that gate until my mate and I are in a position to supervise their passage. If you don't like it you should have been more careful before you came in here bandying four letter words about.' He nods as if nutting the final nail into our coffins and returns to his mate. 'Hang on Fred. Only another half hour to dinner.'

In the end we don't get through the gates until ten past two. Fred does not feel well enough to open the gate until 1231 hours and by that time it is his dinner time. This means that nothing can be done until 1330 hours without offending the rules of the Sedan Chairs And Bedmakers Union — S.C.A.B.s for short — one of the oldest craft unions in the country.

'And very crafty to boot,' says Sid flexing his toe thoughtfully.

At 1331 Fred has a relapse and it takes him another half bottle of brandy to summon up the strength to cross the road. Sid and I aren't allowed to help him because this would obviously interfere with the demarcation agreements. By five past two he and Arthur — that is his thirsty mate — have got the gate unpadlocked, and at ten past, it swings open and knocks an old lady off her bike. This upsets Fred and Arthur so much that they immediately retire to the Workers United to calm their nerves. Sid and I help the old lady on to her bike and drive into the yard. It is noticeable that the car is now without hub caps and has lost its wireless aerial.

'I don't know why you still want to go through with this,' I say. 'I'm amazed this place could afford the advertisement in *The Times.*'

'Shut up, faint-heart!' snaps Sid. 'Can't you see that this is just the kind of challenge I'm itching to grapple with? If I can get this place moving then it will serve as a belitia beacon to the whole of British industry.'

With these proud words he pulls up beside a sign saying 'Parking Reserved For Executive Personnel' under which has been scrawled 'Get stuffed!'. I don't say anything because I am a bit choked about missing dinner. We had a scotch egg in the boozer but it didn't amount to much. I saw a fly walk across it and start cleaning its feet immediately afterwards.

'I wonder where Rightberk is?' says Sid. 'Ah, this sturdy son of toil will no doubt be able to tell us.' I look around the yard but the only person he can be talking about looks as energetic as an attack of sleeping sickness. He glances contemptuously from Sid to the car and then back again as if he cares for neither of them.

'Excuse me,' says Sid preserving the unnaturally polite

manner that has so far been a feature of his visit to U.I.B. 'Can you direct me to Mr Rightberk?'

'You must be desperate for company if you want to see that twat,' says the man in a voice that does not suggest a promising future playing Father Christmas to highly strung children. 'Past the workshops and at the top of the office block. That's where he hangs out when he's not playing golf.'

He slouches on his way and Sid shakes his head. 'Classic example of a breakdown of confidence,' he says. 'We've got to restore this firm's belief in itself.'

It is strange, but though we follow the direction in which the man was pointing a couple of fingers, we do not seem to be passing any workshops. There is a room in which a lot of men are stretched out on beds and another in which groups of men are sitting around playing cards and reading papers. There are some work benches and baulks of timber in the second room but nobody is touching them.

'Must be their dinner break,' says Sid.

'A quarter past two is a bit late to be having dinner, isn't it?' I say.

'It is strange,' agrees Sid. 'Maybe they work staggered shifts.'

'That would figure,' I say. 'Some of them were staggering and they all looked a bit shifty.'

Sid pays little attention to my amusing joke but strides purposefully through the door of the office building and begins to ascend the stairs two at a time. There is a door at the top with a cracked glass panel bearing the name Rightberk followed by a crudely drawn exclamation mark. Beyond the door is an outer office with a desk, typewriter and a wall full of post cards from exotic places such as Sitges, Rimini and my old stamping ground, Cromingham. As we enter, a man backs out of the inner office carrying a set of golf clubs. He is unaware of our presence and addresses someone at floor level.

'Better get your knickers on, Carole. There's just a chance that the mugs might still show up. If it's nice tomorrow I probably won't come in.'

Sid coughs discreetly and the bloke whips round and bashes his nut on the door in a manner that would have drawn a warm glow of approval from Oliver Hardy. He has a clothes-brush moustache that goes through half a dozen shades between dirty brown and off white, a ruddy complexion and a boozer's conk. His eyes are bloodshot and his teeth as yellow as the Chinese football team. All in all, he is quite a riot of colour.

'Mr Rightberk?' Sid does not wait for an answer but steps forward to look into the inner office. I step with him.

There, at floor level, I witness one of the most beautiful sights that can smite the mince pies of man. A luscious dolly is leaning forward to encase her generous knockers in a bra whilst her long pins willow forward invitingly without encumbrance. The lack of cover extends to her minge fringe which quivers invitingly before disappearing behind a modest knee.

'You left one of your balls behind.' Sid reaches between the lady's legs and retrieves a golf ball which he buries in Rightberk's palm.

'Mr Noggett!? What a truly marvellous surprise. We'd given you up for lost. The mugs I was referring to were of course for the office staff's morning coffee. I've noticed quite a lot of chipped cups lately. Most unhygienic. I think mugs will be much sturdier, don't you?'

'They'll probably stand up to a bit more knocking about,' says Sid without taking his eyes off Carol. 'Sorry we're late. We had a bit of trouble getting into the place.' Sid outlines the nature of our problem and Rightberk hurls his golf clubs to the ground ferociously.

'Filthy idle swines!' he snarls. 'Most of them refuse to

clock in unless they get danger money. They're terrified of spraining their wrists when they pull the handle. I don't know why I go on pouring money and time into this business —' He slows up when he sees me nudging Sid — 'not, of course, that there aren't some wonderful pickings to be had. That's what makes it so tragic.'

'Do you have good relations with the unions, here?' asks Sid. Rightberk swallows hard and closes his eyes for a second.

'There's only one union. One of their rules is that you can't have members of any other union in the same building. Our relationship varies from day to day.'

'Do you have a Personnel Manager?' asks Sid.

'He shot himself. I mean—I'm certain it was an accident. He was cleaning his brother-in-law's revolver on the parapet of Tower Bridge.'

'So you handle staff relations?' Carole has now closed the door of the inner office in Sid's face and we both turn and face Rightberk.

'Yes, I do. Of course, it doesn't mean that I wouldn't be prepared to designate if you came into the business.'

'No, of course not.' I can see Sid wondering whether designation stunts your growth.

'You probably noticed that I laid on something for you?' Rightberk jerks his head over his shoulder.

'For *us*?' says Sid

'You didn't put in an appearance so Miss Gotcher and I got down to it.'

'I did wonder,' says Sid.

'Unfortunately, the clotted cream exploded all over her. You know how it can, sometimes?'

'I've seen photographs,' says Sid.

'I don't know if you've had anything, but if you still feel like a nibble there's plenty left.'

I can see that the idea appeals. 'I've never had anything.' Sid turns to me. 'But what about him?'

'I've never had anything either,' I say. I did have this throbbing pain once but it didn't amount to anything.

'Splendid,' says Rightberk. 'Then I'll ask Miss Gotcher to accommodate both of you.'

'Here! Hang on a minute,' says Sid — but it is too late. Mr Rightberk flings open the door of his inner sanctum and waves towards a trolley weighed down with plates of meat — I mean plates of meat, not feet — and trifles and the like.

'Ah, Miss Gotcher,' he says. 'Would you mind catering for these gentlemen's appetites? Have you got those marks off your blouse yet?'

'There's one big one,' she says. 'I don't think it's going to come out.' She gives a little pout when she says that and looks straight into Sid's mince pies. I can see that he could well become putty — or possibly, something more substantial — in her hands.

'Oh I see,' says Sid. 'You laid on some grub for us. That's very kind. I wouldn't say no. Ta.' He gets stuck into a slice of egg pie and nods appreciatively. 'Was this made on the premises?'

Rightberk shakes his head. 'No. The cooking here is of a somewhat fundamental nature to accord with the men's desires. Bungers and mush, that kind of thing.'

'Bangers and mash!' corrects Miss Gotcher.

'Something like that,' says Rightberk airily. He has a very twittish accent and I can see him getting up people's brackets so far that he defoliates them.

'Now,' says Sid. 'Let's talk turkey.'

'The ham is very good as well,' says Rightberk reaching out for the plate.

'I was referring to The Universal International Bedding Company,' says Sid. 'There are one or two things I want to ask—'

But Sid never gets the chance because the outer door bursts open and a man of about fifty wearing a knee-length, beige storeman's coat strides in. He has a droopy moustache and a big nose.

'You won't get away with it!' he says.

Rightberk looks at his visitor coldly. 'I didn't know you had an appointment, Mr Umbrage?'

'I don't need one when the workers' interests are being massacred, do I? Do you realise that the labour force were locked in during their dinner hour. They were unable to purchase those small remedial articles which ease their passage through this moving vale of tears.'

'I heard about the incident,' says Rightberk. 'Mr Noggett and his assistant were unable to gain access to the factory because those two drink-sodden geriatrics you insist on us employing were incapable of opening the gates.'

'The men will be paid double time for the hour and a half they were detained against their will or the whole factory comes out. We're not slave labour, you know.'

'It wasn't the fault of the management,' bleats Rightberk.

'Nothing is the fault of the management,' says Umbrage sarcastically. 'You're too busy pigging it up here to care about what happens to the workers.'

'Excuse me,' says Sid. Unfortunately, he has a mouthful of egg pie at the time and he spits it all over Umbrage's coat. Umbrage looks down at the little bits of white and yellow and an expression of extreme distaste spreads across his mug. 'I'm sorry,' continues Sid. 'What I wanted to say is that I sympathise with your problems.'

'You chose a funny way to do it,' says Umbrage.

'I know there's right and wrong on both sides,' says Sid. 'None of us is perfect and there's nothing that can't be settled by us getting together round a table.'

'Wait a minute! Wait a minute!' says Umbrage. 'Who's negotiating for management now, then? You got yourself a new boy, have you, Mr Rightberk?' He stresses each syllable of the name to get the best out of it.

'I think that maybe I had better explain Mr Noggett's position,' says Rightberk, putting down his golf clubs. 'You see—'

'Oh, Mr Rightberk, sir. May I have a word with you?' The speaker who has just burst into the room is wearing a blue pin stripe suit and a harassed expression.

'What is it, Twitterton?' says Rightberk wearily. 'Can't you see that I'm up to my eyes?'

'Sorry, sir. But it's about the "Our policy is one of continuous improvement" signs.'

'What about them, Twitterton?'

'They keep falling off the beds, sir.'

'Twitterton is one of our management trainees,' explains Rightberk as if he doesn't go overboard for the idea. 'A very keen lad.'

'Is Mr Twitterton levelling a charge of incompetence against the operatives in question?' says Umbrage menacingly.

'Of course not, of course not,' says Rightberk jovially.

'But they told me to—' Twitterton checks himself and glances nervously at Miss Gotcher. 'I don't like to say in front of a lady. I think it's a pretty poor show if we can't—'

'Quite, quite,' interrupts Rightberk. 'Very praiseworthy concern but I don't think we need worry too much. It says on the signs that we reserve the right to make changes without giving notice, doesn't it?'

'Yes, but—'

'Right. From now on we don't have the signs.'

'Wait a minute!' growls Umbrage. 'Are you suggesting a course of action that could lead to redundancies?'

'Very well, we'll continue as we are. The signs fall off

after a while. We'll make it part of our "Built In Obsolescence" programme.'

'In that case the men will want a bonus for creative craftsmanship,' says Umbrage firmly.

Mr Rightberk's reaction to that suggestion is never made known to us because a spotty youth wearing a dirty white overall runs into the office. 'The professor's floating down the river!' he gasps.

'Oh my God!' Rightberk kicks his golf clubs savagely and hurls the ball Sid gave him into the corner of the room. 'Can't I ever get any thinking time around here? What is the old fool up to now?'

'One of the water beds broke away from its mooring,' says the youth.

'Water beds?' says Sid.

Rightberk turns to him as if he had temporarily forgotten that he was there. 'Oh yes. Marvellous invention. The ultimate in comfort. You feel as if you're floating on water. Just one or two little bugs to iron out and then we go into production.' He winks at Sid conspiratorially.

'How does it work?' says Sid.

'Well, first of all, you fill your bedroom with water. Not right to the top of course, because then you wouldn't be able to breathe. Then—'

'He's disappearing under Vauxhall Bridge.' Miss Gotcher is peering out of the window.

'Damn,' says Rightberk. 'I'll have to tell you later. We'd better go and retrieve the — the old — er, chap.'

We are all springing for the door when it flies open and a large blonde with a bright red mouth hurtles into the room.

'Lunch all right?' she chirps cheerfully.

Rightberk kisses her long and earnest on the cheek. 'Super. Can't stop, I've got to fish someone out of the drink. Somebody will give you a hand to clear away.'

He looks pointedly at me and Sid takes the hint. 'Be of assistance to the lady, Timothy,' he says, like he registered the way Rightberk referred to me as his assistant. 'I will confer with you later.'

'As thou wilt, mighty one,' I say. 'Take care that your bonce does not get wedged in the door as you go out.'

Sid chooses to ignore that remark and sweeps down the stairs followed by Rightberk, Umbrage and the youth. I notice that Rightberk picks up his golf clubs before leaving.

'I don't think I know you,' says the new bird. 'I'm Prudence Packer. I supply this lot with lunches and assorted goodies.'

'Just them?' I ask.

'No. I service a number of clients. My, my, you've hardly touched my lovely quiche.'

I don't know what her lovely quiche is but she has a number of items I would be delighted to touch. Delicious knockers and a beautifully curved pair of back bumpers that would snuggle into the palms of your hands like a couple of melons. I can just imagine their warm, rounded weight playing pat-a-cake with my marble bag.

'Mr Noggett didn't arrive in time for lunch,' says Miss Gotcher. 'That meant there was rather a lot to finish. In fact, we didn't really start, if you know what I mean — or rather, Mr Rightberk started . . .'

'You don't have to tell me,' says Prudence. 'I got stuck here with him one afternoon when you were on holiday. He just wouldn't let me go. He kept saying that it was a pity you weren't here as well.'

'He's said that to me before now,' says Carole. 'About you, I mean. He obviously fancies a bit of troilism.'

'I wouldn't mind, myself,' says Prudence, almost wistfully. 'But it would have to be with the right person.'

'Or people,' says Carole. She looks at the front of my

trousers. 'Shall we start taking them down?'

I am just trying to remember whether I put on a clean pair of underpants when I realise she is talking about the nosh.

'No hurry,' says Prudence. 'I wouldn't mind having a bite myself. I've been rushing about all morning.'

'I'll join you,' says Carole. 'We won't be seeing my boss again today. I might as well relax a little.' She picks up a bottle of white wine and turns to me. 'Do you like Reisling?'

'I don't know,' I tell her. 'I've never reisled.'

Both girls laugh and Prudence shakes her head. 'Is that original?' she says.

'In a way,' I say. 'You know what it's like.' It is only then that I grab a butchers at the bottle and see that it has "Reisling" written on it. Ho, ho. What a comical caper to be sure. I missed a lot by not having a classical education. 'Yes, a glass of wine would slip down a treat,' I say.

Carole tilts the bottle and I take a good look at the front of her blouse. I can't see any sign of a stain.

'Your blouse looks as if it's going to be all right,' I say. A faint blush deepens the colour of Carole's cheek. 'Have some meringue,' she says.

'What happened to your shirt?' Prudence is perking up and taking interest.

'An attack of the Jeremy Rightberks.' Carole shrugs her shoulders. 'It's not much but it's better than catching up with the filing.'

'Your in-trays are groaning, darling.'

'They're not the only ones.'

I take a large bite out of my meringue and cream squirts all over the front of my shirt. Knickers! Just when I wanted to come over all sophisticated in front of these emancipated birds.

'Oh dear. Look what's happened,' says Prudence.

'Have you got a cloth?' I say. 'It's all right. I don't think any of it has gone on the carpet.'

'We don't want to waste it.'

Before I can shout for help, Carole has dropped to her knees and slid her arms round my waist. Opening her mouth wide she begins to suck up the cream from my chest and dig her fingers into the small of my back. Down at crotch level, Percy stirs like a restless sea fanned by a wind of promise. Carole raises her head so that she can pluck open the buttons of my shirt and I draw her creamy mouth on to mine and wipe it against my lips. I don't know much about nutrition but this isn't half a good way to supplement your calorie intake.

Carole's hands drop down between my legs and as I fondle beneath her skirt I peer up to where Prudence is looking down on us.

'Let's turn this into a gastronomic occasion,' she says.

For a moment I think she means that she is going to be sick and then tugs up her T-shirt and rakes my minces with her bristols as she pulls the garment over her head. She is wearing a bra but this hits the deck faster than an Italian war hero hearing a car backfire.

'You like cream, don't you?'

Sensitive readers should stop right here. I wouldn't believe it myself unless it was actually happening to me. Miss Packer picks up a carton of whipped cream and pops a couple of generous pats on to her paps. Without further ado or a pause for the weather forecast — gale force erections approaching from a southerly direction — she slaps one of her mammarial appurtenances up against my cakehole and awaits developments. Fortunately, I have been in enough sticky situations to know how to cloak my shock and when I open my mouth to protest and a cream coated knocker is thrust into it I am able to put a good face on it. This I do for several minutes whilst at crotch level, my action man kit gets up to tricks that would make a Bisto Kid turn in his gravy. Miss Gotcher has not been slow to learn the combination that holds up my trousers and has withdrawn my prize with every sign of satisfaction.

'Gorgeous,' she says, reaching behind her for the cream carton. 'If there's one thing I really fancy it's a banana split.'

CHAPTER THREE

In which Timmy joins the work force of Slumbernog and experiences the strange ritual of 'Nut Squidging' in the Stuffing Department. Also in which he attends a union meeting and is introduced to the mysteries of the Cuddle Chamber — a bed-testing centre.

'You all right?' says Sid. 'You look a bit pale.'

'I think I must have eaten something that agreed with me,' I say.

Sid shakes his head. 'You mean that didn't *agree* with you, you twerp.'

'Have it your own way, Sid. How did you make out with the professor?'

Sid adopts his reverential expression, usually reserved for anybody who has made a lot of money. 'A wonderful man,' he says. 'A bit eccentric but definitely a genius. That bed of his is really something. You know, he was fast asleep when we caught up with him. Once we solve the leakage problem I think we've got ourselves a winner.'

'You mean, the leakage problem in relation to the bed?'

'No. In relation to the room you put it in. Usually the water flows under the door and down the stairs. Even if you leave all the taps on it doesn't seem to keep pace. Then there's the problem with the electricity — and the neighbours —'

'Sid,' I interrupted him. 'Does this mean that you're seriously considering going in with these idiots? Why not just set fire to the money? That way you could warm your hands on it for a few moments and it wouldn't be completely wasted.'

Sid puts on his misunderstood genius expression. 'Ignoring with difficulty your tasteless sarcasm, I have to concede that there were moments when I wondered whether this proposition represented the apogee of investment potential. Nevertheless, upon due consideration of the facts as they have been placed before me I have come to the conclusion that the presence of Professor Nuttibarm is sufficient to outweigh the more deliterious aspects of the operation.'

'When you put it like that I find it hard to disagree with you,' I say. 'What were you talking about?'

'I was saying that old Nuttibarm is shit hot,' says Sid. 'You should see some of the things he's come up with. There's a special bed for fakirs. The nails are controlled by magnets so that they can rearrange them into whatever position makes them feel most uncomfortable.'

'Hardly a mass market line,' I say.

'Then there's the bed that's suspended by chains from the ceiling. Very restful and dead easy for sweeping under. You have to be careful what you do in it, though. There was this couple who started having a bit of the other and battered their way through into the next door flat.'

'I wouldn't fancy that,' I say. 'Hasn't he got anything a bit simpler?'

'He's not interested in simple things, Timmo. He's after the bed of the future. For instance, you know what a blooming nuisance it is when you feel like a piss in the middle of the night and you're tucked up all snug and comfortable?'

'Only too well, Sid. When you get downstairs you find that someone has left the karsi window open and your knackers nearly freeze off.'

'Exactly. Well, you want the Commodoor. You press a button in the side and it opens down the middle so that you can do your business without getting out of bed.'

'You need to have special sheets, I suppose?'

'Oh yes, and they haven't quite ironed out all the bugs yet.'

'Bed bugs, Sid?'

'Watch it, Timmo! There's one or two safety factors got

to be built in. There was this other couple having a bit of the other — or it may have been the same one, I don't know. Anyway, the tart gets a bit carried away and presses the button by mistake. WOMP! The bed opens and they end up on the floor.'

'Very nasty, Sid. It could dent your confidence, couldn't it?'

'Not as nasty as the bloke who was actually using the thing when his old woman turned on the bedside lamp to find a pair of earplugs or something.'

'What happened, Sid?'

'She pressed the closure switch by mistake.'

'No, Sid!'

'I'm afraid so. The neighbours said they hadn't heard a scream like it since the tom cat caught its tail in the mangle.'

'Cut off in his prime, was he?'

'No, but he's got a long thin one and his voice is inclined to break after the second pint.'

Sid starts to tell me some more of Professor Nuttibarm's wonderful ideas but I tell him I've had enough. I always thought bed was a nice gentle place. At U.I.B. it seems more like an extension of World War Two — and the BBC must have gone as far as you can go with that.

'All right,' says Sid. 'You'll be finding out for yourself soon enough. You start working your way through the departments tomorrow.'

'Tomorrow, Sid! That's a bit sudden, isn't it?'

'No!' shouts Sid. 'You've got to plunge in and seize the bull by the short and curlies otherwise you might as well not bother. I'm starting tomorrow.'

'And what are you going to do?'

'I'm going up to London with Jeremy to buy myself a set of golf clubs.'

'Golf clubs!?'

'It's never worth sneering at things you don't really understand.' says Sid loftily. 'Jeremy told me that most top level negotiations are done on the golf course. It's a business convention. I owe it to my fellow employees to become effete with the game.'

'"Au fait" not "effete",' I tell him. "Effete means washed out, feeble — I don't know, though. Maybe you were right the first time.'

'Anyway, I'm not going up just for the golf clubs,' says Sid. 'I'm signing a few papers and having luncheon — that's what you call dinner.'

'Oh Sid! I can see you being taken for a terrible ride if you're not careful. What's happened to all that shop floor stuff? I thought you wanted to be shoulder to shoulder with the workers?'

'I am!' says Sid bitterly. 'In the mind. It's not possible for me to get down there physically and at the same time oversee the whole operation. I've got to take the broad view. I'm going to be with you in spirit just as much as if I was toiling at a lathe.'

'Sid. Before you sign anything. Are you sure that this is the right proposition?' Nobody can say that I am not trying to save the poor mut, can they?

Sidney taps his hooter. 'Trust my conk,' he says. 'I've got an instinct for this kind of thing.' That is rather like a lemming saying that it fancies itself as a long distance swimmer and I decide to give up. If Sid wants to chuck his money down the drain, that is his business.

I am told to clock in at eight the next morning so at ten to I am looking for my card in the rack and by five to I am ready for work. Mr Umbrage, who is foreman as well as shop steward, is going to look after me. By one minute to, nobody has shewn up and when I hear eight o'clock striking I think that I must have arrived on a public holiday by mistake. I am just about to turn away when there is a rushing noise like the beating of hundreds of pairs of wings, and a mass of blokes and bints flood through the gateway. Shouting and cursing at each other they jostle for position around the clocking-in machine and the handle goes up and down like it is on the village pump. By one minute past eight, everybody has disappeared again.

What I find a bit surprising is that nobody has actually gone into the factory. Once they have clocked in, they do a smart about turn and cross the road in the direction of Alf's Cafe. Not so much 'in the direction of', more straight through the front door. Oh well, if I want to avoid being lonely I had better follow them. Perhaps Mr Umbrage will be there.

Mr Umbrage is indeed there. Tucked in behind a cup of tea and the *Daily Sun* — "Convent girl confesses all in new, horror, shock, drama — exclusive!" I feel knackered just reading the headline. Mr U seems deeply engrossed in his paper so I deem it diplomatic to join the queue wending its way to the counter.

'Are we on a go slow today?' says the bloke in front of me to his mate.

'I dunno. I get confused,' says the bloke. 'Better ask the Commissar.' He nods towards Umbrage. 'Not that it makes any bleeding difference. Last bleeding strike we had, it took bleeding management two bloody weeks to realise what had happened.'

I order a cup of cha and a wad and sit down opposite Umbrage who is still hidden behind his newspaper. After a few moments he makes a quiet chuckling noise and puts the paper down. I see that he has been looking at a photo of a naked tart wearing a sailor's titfer. 'The broad bosom of the ocean' reads the caption.

The smile on Umbrage's face dies when he sees me. 'Oh,' he says. 'It's the nark. Where have you been?'

'I was waiting by the clocking in machine,' I say.

'Eager to start clawing your way to the top, eh?' sneers Umbrage.

'No. I thought that's where you'd expect to find me.'

'Well, you were wrong!' hisses Umbrage. 'We fought and slaved for the privilege of preparing for our toil and it's not something we intend to relinquish in a hurry. If they had their way —' Umbrage waves an accusing finger towards the ceiling as if Rightberk and his ilk are squatting on the lamp bracket '— we'd be driven through those gates like sheep and lashed to the benches. You wouldn't have time to take your cycle clips off.' He pauses and glares at me as if daring me to say something. I note that the ends of his moustache are bedraggled where he dunked them in his tea. 'I'm assigning you to the wharf with Lenny and Harry. And, don't forget — I've got your number.'

'Oh thank you,' I say, trying to sound pleased. 'What is it? I thought that thing on my time card was my number.'

'Don't take the piss with me, Sonny!' Umbrage waggles his finger under my nose. 'I know what you're up to. Reporting back to the bosses. Well, you watch it. We've had experience of your sort before. The last informer had a very nasty accident when the roof of a four poster fell on him.'

'I'll do my best,' I say.

'Never mind about that,' says Umbrage. 'You just do what you're paid to do.' With these words, he rises to his feet and strolls majestically towards the door. Before going out he has a word with a bloke playing dominoes and the man comes over to me.

'I'm, Lenny,' he says. He indicates the man he is playing dominoes with. 'He's Harry. You're with us.'

'Fine,' I say. 'When do we start?'

'Start what?'

'Work,' I say.

Immediately, an ugly silence falls over the room and Lenny looks embarrassed. 'We have started,' he says. 'It's twenty past eight.'

I am about to say something and then I think better of it. Obviously, there is something about this word that gives rise to deep-seated resentment.

'Do you want me to do anything?' I say.

'Just sit there till we've finished. Then we'll enrol you in the union and we can go over to the wharf.'

'Do I have to join the union?' I ask.

Lenny looks horrified. 'Of course you do. It wouldn't be right for you to take advantage of all the benefits won by the union if you didn't pay your sub, would it?'

'I take advantage of a lot of things in life that I personally haven't been responsible for.'

The bloke behind the counter starts to move cups and saucers out of the way.

Lenny looks at Harry who shakes his head. 'Are you saying that you don't want to join the union?' he asks.

'I'm not quite certain,' I say.

'Let me put it this way,' says Harry. 'If you don't join we'll chuck you through that window.'

'I'll join,' I say. 'Nobody explained it to me properly before.'

I sign the necessary piece of paper and receive a yellow booklet which is a combination of my membership card and thousands of little spaces which are filled in whenever I pay my union dues. I hand over 20p, Lenny and Harry finish their game of dominoes, the clock strikes nine o'clock and we are ready to go. Lenny gives me a dignified nod and rises to his feet, Harry flicks his head towards the door, and I practically hear The Dambusters' March. You don't have to be a writhing mass of sentiment to respond at a moment like that — but it helps.

'Watch out for the nut squidging!' The voice at my side is so soft that it takes me a moment to hear what it is saying.

'What—?' I begin, but Lenny turns round and the slim beturbanned figure at my side drifts away. No, it is not Jungle Boy. It is clearly an attractive bint bent upon giving me a warning. 'Nut squidging'? It does not ring a bell. I know that in the old days, apprentices were subjected to some pretty rough treatment when joining a firm, but surely—

'We'll take a short cut through the stuffing department. You might as well see what you're going to be up against on Tolpuddle day.' Lenny pushes open a door and I find myself amongst a bevy of birds who are engaged in manipulating long strips of foam rubber into mattress covers stretched out on metal frames. For some reason it reminds me of stuffing chickens. Quite a few of the birds are a lot easier on the minces than a clench of digits and I notice that my appearance caused a ripple of what can only be called interest to pass through their ranks. Nice to know that the old animal magnetism is still coursing through my fortunate veins.

'You want to watch yourself here, Tim,' says Harry. 'They're a bit wild some of these girls. All that stuffing goes to their heads.'

Whilst I am enlarging upon this interesting thought, I am clocking the little darling who tipped me the wink in Alf's Cafe. She has just come into the room and her expression of impending disaster would feel at home on the mush of any expert examining Britain's trade figures. She seems to be pushing me backwards with her eyes. 'Nut squidging?' What could she have meant?

'Never come in here with less than a couple of mates,' says Lenny. 'It's the only place where the union can't protect you.'

'Especially at Christmas time,' says Harry with a shudder. 'Last year they stripped that Twitterton bloke naked and hung him up instead of mistletoe.'

It is funny to hear them talk like that because they look a nice bunch of girls. You wouldn't think there was a blow job amongst them.

'Do they just stuff the mattresses?' I ask.

'They assemble some of the beds,' says Lenny. 'See that bird over there with the mouthful of washers and nuts?'

'The one looking at us?'

'She's looking at you, Tim. You must have made a hit there.'

'Run for it!' Harry obviously knows his way around the stuffing room.

'Squidge his nuts!'

Upon consideration, I reckon that those three words could have brought an end to the dearth of British track gold medals at the last few Olympic Games. If they can have this effect on fifty-year-old men, just think what they could have done for a fully trained athlete. Lenny and Harry must touch 80 mph as they accelerate through the door at the far end of the work room. I try to follow them but the words obviously don't have the same magic for me — not then, they don't. Before I have fully appreciated what is happening, I have been surrounded by crumpet.

'Morning,' I say brightly, treating them to a quick flash of my Teds. 'Everything all right then?'

Those are the last words that I can remember speaking till I find myself in the corridor. Like a pack of ravenous beasts the birds hurl themselves at me and proceed to lay rude hands on the front of my trousers. At first I think it is some kind of jest but then I find that they mean business — one of the few things at U.I.B. that does. Sheer weight of numbers bears me to the ground and I can feel my trousers being tugged down to my ankles. It is all very childish and

— OUCH!! Somebody has grabbed hold of Percy like he is an escaping gerbil. This is too much! What do they think they're — OUCH!!I twist myself into a position to see what is happening at fun palace level and find that a large washer is being slipped over my tonk.

Five minutes and a lot of struggling, later, I have forty-eight washers and a nut turning my hampton into a piece of modern jewellery. Unfortunately, in the course of all the messing about, Percy has begun to respond with his usual coarse and undiscriminating vigour and there seems no chance of the washers ever coming off. It looks as if I will have to go down to the fire station, though I don't fancy some geezer starting to mess about with a hack saw — on second thoughts, forget it. I will have to go through life like one of those African women who wear all those rings round their necks. Provided rust doesn't set in too early I should be all right. I suppose you could say that it will add a bit of lustre to my cluster.

My attitude to this brutal assault may seem strangely philosophical but it does not take me long to adjust to the personality of a place and I can sense that the Universal International Bedding Centre — or Slumbernog as it probably is by now — is something apart from your run-of-the-mill, small South London business venture. After the treatment I received at the hands — and other things — of Carole Gotcher and Prudence Packer, having a few washers bunged on your cock is kid's stuff. At least they didn't put my old man in a vice to do it.

I stagger along the corridor and follow the sign that says 'Wharf! Wharf!' Once the girls had finished putting the nut on my dick they let me go without further ado. I didn't have to make a bolt for it — bolt for it? Get it? Oh well, please yourselves.

Lenny and Harry are looking down into the water as I approach. Although a barge full of timber is waiting to be unloaded there is no indication that they have soiled their nicotine-stained fingers with gruelling labour before my arrival.

'Are you all right?' says Lennie. 'We could hear you chinking down the corridor a hundred yards away. Sorry we didn't hang about but my back isn't what it used to be.'

'My insides have been playing up something rotten lately,' says Harry. They both make self-excusing groaning noises and feel different parts of their bodies. A washer drops out of one of my trouserlegs and rolls across the floor.

'How many?' Says Harry.

'Forty-eight, I think,' I say.

'That's a new record, isn't it?' says Lennie. 'Mind you, we have changed over to metric, haven't we?'

'Started to change,' says Harry. 'They're phasing it in. Blooming silly if you ask me. It's like when they changed over to left hand driving in Ireland. They gave everybody a week to practice.'

Four more washers roll across the floor and I sense that things are loosening up at lollipop level.

'Right,' says Lennie. 'Better get down to it, hadn't we?' He flexes his arms and immediately lets out a sharp yelp of pain. Twenty minutes later, the spasm has passed and he feels well enough to continue — or start, depending on which way you look at it.

'What do we have to do?' I say.

'When the bloke on the barge puts the wood on the wharf we put it on the pallett and the bloke on the fork lift truck takes it away.'

'Got it,' I say. I put a foot on the barge and Harry reacts as if I have trodden on his face.

'Are you mad? That's not your job. If all that timber falls on you, you're not covered.'

'Really?' I say.

'Yeah. Bleeding really. You leave the unloading to the bloke on the barge. That's what he gets paid for. Right, mate?'

'Right.' The bloke on the barge tips his cap on to the back of his head and slowly climbs to his feet.

'Right,' says Lenny.

'Right,' says Harry.

'Right,' I say.

'Who asked you?' says Harry.

Half an hour later, three loads of timber have been deposited on the quay and we have built a crude shelter with them.

'It can get very parky out here when the sun goes in,' explains Lenny. 'And about six o'clock the wind comes up.'

'Six o'clock?' I say. 'What are you doing here then?'

'Over-time,' says Harry. 'The job's not worth a light without over-time. A man couldn't survive on what they pay for a day's work at this place.'

'So that's why we're spinning it out, is it?' I ask.

'Spinning it out? What are you on about? We're just trying to get the job done in our own time. "Have a go and have a blow." That's the S.C.A.B.s motto.'

It is eleven o'clock before we begin to load the first pallett and the geezer on the fork lift truck has finished doing *The Times* crossword and fallen asleep at his machine. The three of us never work at the same time. Two men toil while the third 'has a blow'.

At five past eleven I have an idea. 'If the wood was loaded on to palletts in the first place, then it could be taken straight off by the fork lift truck,' I say brightly.

'Oh yes?' Lenny looks at Harry and nods his head slowly.

'Do you want to put that in the suggestion box?' says Harry.

'Do you think it's a good idea?' I say.

'It's a bleeding good idea if you want to be out of a job!' accuses Lenny. 'You want to shut your mouth before you say things like that. What are you? Some kind of trouble maker? Umby told us to watch out for you.'

'I was just trying to make things easier,' I say.

'Easier for the bosses!' snaps Harry. 'They'd have the whole place run by a couple of machines if they could. You don't want to give them a chance to make any more cuts in the labour force.'

'I'm sorry,' I say. 'I won't say anything about it.'

'You'd better not do, otherwise we'll have to tell Mr Umbrage we can't work with you. That reminds me. What's the time?'

'Eleven fifteen.'

'Right, we'd better get going. There's a union meeting at half past.'

'Do all the meetings take place during working hours?' I ask.

'All except the elections.'

'Is that when Mr Umbrage gets elected?'

'That's right.'

'How many votes did he get in by?' I ask.

'I don't know. I've never been to one of those meetings. Have you, Harry?'

'I should cocoa! After work? You must be joking.'

Since we had a fifteen minute tea break at ten o'clock that lasted twenty-five minutes it can be seen that the sweat is not exactly pouring off me as I walk towards the staff canteen. It is a funny thing, but the less I do, the more tired I get. I was quite chipper after the nut squidging, now, I feel knackered.

'Are you all right? I tried to warn you.' The quiet little voice is at my side again. I look down and see the bird who tipped me off about the 'nut squidging'. She is very skinny with big eyes like one of those things that hangs upside down from trees— marmitesets, or whatever they are.

'I'm fine.' Another washer rolls across the yard. 'Well, not bad. As well as can be expected in the circumstances. I'm sorry I didn't understand what you were on about.'

'I'm sorry I couldn't tell you more clearly but they were all looking at me. They're really nasty some of them. They fitted a chastity belt to one girl just before she got married. It wouldn't have been so bad if they hadn't thrown away the key.'

I try and look sympathetic. It is obvious that this bint has a soft spot for yours truly and you never know when one might come in handy. 'That's terrible,' I say. 'I don't mind a bit of horseplay but you can go too far.'

'Quite.' The bird gazes up at me through big goo, goo eyes and I wonder how far would be too far as far as she is concerned.

'What's your name?' she says.

'Timothy Lea.'

'Jean,' she says. She obviously doesn't reckon her second name a lot.

'Do you like working here?' I say, thinking that I might as well get a bird's eye view of the place.

'It's all right.' Her enthusiasm does not reach epidemic proportions. 'I don't know how long it's going to last, though.'

'What's the trouble?' I say, pricking up my ears.

'I have a friend who works in sales and she says there aren't any.'

My heart sinks. Typical. Once again the dead hand of Noggett lights upon another stone-cold loser.

'No stock?'

'No customers. There's a yard full of frames out the back and they don't know where to put the mattresses that are piling up.'

The full dimension of the problem comes home to me. If the efforts of Harry and Lenny are an indication of the rate of output achieved by the Slumbernog work force then it must require a quite remarkable lack of enthusiasm for the end product before stock can actually begin to pile up.

'What do you think the problem is?' I say. We are passing the room full of beds with blokes lying on them and as I watch some of them begin to stretch and fold up their newspapers. I imagine that they must be coming to the meeting too.

'It's difficult to put your finger on it.' Another washer rolls across the yard and we both look the other way. I reckon there must be about forty-two left, now. 'The management don't know what they're doing and the union wouldn't let them do it if they did know.'

'What about Professor Nuttibarm?'

'He's the worst of the lot. I don't think we've ever sold anything he's designed.'

I groan inwardly. So much for Sidney's secret weapon. My brother-in-law would enter a tap dancing contest in a pair of deep sea diver's boots.

'What are they doing in there?' I say for a little light relief, indicating the blokes on the beds.

'That's the bed testing department. The union is very hot on that. No bed is allowed to leave the factory until it has been tested for two weeks.'

'They just lie on them, do they?' I ask.

Jean blushes in a way that I find not unattractive. 'Tests of a more personal nature are performed in the Cuddle Chamber,' she says as if reading from a brochure. 'You have to be married to take part.'

'That's a pity,' I say, ravishing her with my roguish eyes. 'Where is the Cuddle Chamber?'

'Over there,' she says. I follow her quivering digit and see a corrugated iron shed that looks as if it has been used as a Pioneer Corps Naafi. Even as I watch, the whole structure starts to shudder and shake and two sheets of corrugated iron fall off the roof to be added to those scattered over a wide area. For a moment I think that I must be experiencing some kind of heat haze because the edges of the building turn fuzzy. It must be the speed at which the walls are reverberating.

'They're testing now,' says Jean. Her tiny frame starts to shiver in time with the shed and it occurs to me that her heart — not to mention the more succulent parts of her body — may well lie within its walls.

As I ponder about the kind of creatures that can manufacture so much rapture, the building jumps six inches out of its foundations, two window frames fall out and there is the sound of collapsing metal.

'Reject!!' bellows a familiar voice.

As I try and think who it can be, the dust settles and the front door starts to open and then topples off its hinges. Framed in the opening is Mr Umbrage. His damp hair is matted over his eyes and one side of his moustache goes up in the air like that Spanish painter bloke — Salvolatile Daily or whatever his name is. Umbrage fastens the buckle of his thick leather belt and, swelling his chest, adopts a heroic stance and shakes one fist towards the sky. 'Up the workers!' he shouts.

I am still thinking about it when he skips off and disappears through the door of what I imagine must be the canteen. In his place emerges a tall blonde woman, looking about her nervously and trying to smooth down the front of her crumpled dress. Jean sucks in her breath sharply.

'OOOer!' she says. 'You know who that is?'

'Search me,' I say.

Jean examines the means of access to my body and for a second I think that she may be taking me seriously. 'Mrs

Rightberk!' she breathes, finally.

'So you don't have to be married to use the Cuddle Chamber,' I say, fixing her with one of my beady orbs. 'That's worth remembering, isn't it?'

'You are awful!' she says. She sounds about as genuine as two birds kissing each other.

I am on the point of volunteering for a quick spot of bed testing when a geezer sticks his head out of the door Umbrage disappeared through and beckons us to get a move on.

'We don't want to cut into our dinner hour,' he says.

Inside the room there are about a hundred men and women sitting on benches and facing a platform behind which sits Umbrage, flanked by two blokes and a bird. As we enter, Umbrage rises to his feet.

'Greetings brothers and sisters,' he says. 'This extraordinary general meeting of the Sedan Chair And Bedmakers Union has been called to draw your attention to a number of outrages which have been perpetrated against you, the downtrodden workers, and to decide what collective retribution should be levelled against those who seek to exploit you.'

'Hear, Hear,' says the bloke sitting on Umbrage's left.

'Did I hear a collective murmer of assent run round the hall?' says Umbrage.

Nobody says anything. Umbrage turns to his left and his mate stands up. 'All those in favour of a collective murmur of assent running round the hall, raise their right hand.' Everybody obediently raises their hand. 'Carried unanimously.'

'Thank you.' Umbrage gives a satisfied nod. 'Basically, I am disturbed on your behalf by the abysmal rates of pay accorded to those men engaged in the arduous chore of bed testing. Not only is there the immediate physical danger of one of the legs dropping off just about the same time that they are, but there are the longer term effects. I refer of course to the unhappy plight of those men who spend so much time asleep at work that they cannot sleep when they get home. They roam the house uneasily, make endless cups of cocoa and are driven to reading the articles in the TV magazines.' There are shouts of 'No!' and 'How horrible!' from the floor. 'Yes, brothers and sisters! And that is just the thin end of the wedge. Some of the poor unfortunates have taken to squandering their hard won earnings on model aeroplane kits. They sit there to the early hours of the morning trying to conjure up Mark I Spitfires until the smell of the balsa wood glue drives them to fits of rapacity unequalled since the days of Attila the Hun! Sweeping the frail fragments of polished wood to the floor they stampede up the stairs and wreak their sleepless lust on the ill-prepared bodies of their dear ones dreaming of pillow cases full of Greenshield stamps!!' Umbrage pauses for breath and all around me, men and women start leaping to their feet and shouting 'One out, all out!' 'It's a scandal!' 'Send them round to me!!' and other meaningless phrases.

Obviously satisfied with the effect his words are having, Umbrage takes a sip from the glass of water in front of him and holds up a hand for silence. 'I can see, brothers and sisters, that you agree with me that this disgusting state of affairs should no longer be allowed to continue. With your concurrence, my executive and I are proposing to management, in the strongest possible terms, that all bed testing work should be undertaken at time and a half rate except when it becomes overtime or weekend work. In the latter eventuality the rate then increases pro rata. Is there anyone who understands what I'm saying?'

One hand rises slowly into the air.

'Then belt up, Smart Alec! Right. We'll take a vote on it. All those in favour?' A forest of hands goes up. 'Carried unanimously. Now, since nobody knows the words of "The Red Flag" and they sound a bit daft anyway, we'll all sing "For He's a Jolly Good Fellow Traveller".'

'Oh Brother Umbrage.' Umbrage seems surprised to find himself accosted from the body of the hall but leans forward indulgently.

'Yes, Heckmondwyke?'

'What about the Labour Day celebrations, this year?'

Umbrage smiles tolerantly. 'I was going to mention that, brother. But thank you for asking —'

'I'm sorry, brother. I wouldn't have interrupted if I'd known.'

'That's quite all right, brother. It doesn't matter.'

'I wouldn't have said anything if —'

'Shut up, you stupid old git!!' Umbrage waits to see if he is going to need to squeeze off the second barrel and then relaxes. 'What I was about to say concerns our annual pilgrimage to Tolpuddle, home of the ill-fated martyrs whose heroic sacrifices sowed the seeds of the great trade union movement. You, like me, I know, have returned from this trip purged and refreshed as by a visit to a religious monument. However owing to the cost of the coach to Dorset and complaints about the teas, we have decided this year to go to Southend.' A whoop of joy rises from the audience. 'Thank you, brothers and sisters. It is indeed encouraging to us on the executive to know that the reward of our toil is your approval. At this moment we are trying to fix up the first leg of an exchange visit with a group of brothers and sisters from the Worker's Paradise — or Soviet Union as it is called by the capitalist press — and I will give you more details of this when our representative at the Anglo Russian Friendship Society returns from her holiday at Bournemouth. And now, let us rise to our feet and —'

After a couple of choruses of 'For He's A Jolly Good

Fellow Traveller', the meeting breaks up and Jean and I join the throng struggling for the exit.

'I can see what Mrs Rightberk sees in him,' says Jean wistfully. 'His revolutionary fervour gets me going.'

'You mean Umbrage?' I say. It really does take me a minute to realise who she is talking about.

'Of course. He sat next to me on the coach once.'

'Listen,' I say, taking a quick shufti at the corrugated iron shack to see that it is still standing. 'Why don't you and I pop over to the Cuddle Chamber and get better acquainted?' Now that Umbrage has got her going it seems a pity not to take advantage of it.

'Are you mad?' she says. 'This is my lunch hour.'

Another washer rolls out of my trouser leg and I kick it savagely in the direction of the canteen.

CHAPTER FOUR

In which Timmy attends a Board Meeting at the A.C.D.C. ('Artisan Controllers' Dining Club) and meets Plantagenet, Maitland, Henry and Crispin Rightberk. Also, some topless waitresses who perform unusual services for their customers below tablecloth level.

'How's it going then?' I say. It is a few days after the union meeting and I am having a drink with Sid in the Highwayman. I have hardly clapped eyes on him at the factory.

'Not bad,' he says. 'My approach shots are all right but I'm dead ropey off the tee.'

It takes me a few moments to realise what he is on about. 'Golf?' I say. 'Is that where you've been?'

'It gets a grip of you,' says Sid earnestly. 'Even if I wasn't doing it for the firm I'd still be dead keen. The other day — it was funny, really — I'd just sliced my drive into this little wood—'

'Copse,' I say.

'Where?' Sid looks round nervously.

'I was referring to the little wood, not the fuzz,' I say derisively. 'Gordon Bennett. What are you wasting your time playing golf for? Why aren't you back at the factory? That's where you're needed. The whole place is about to collapse.'

'First things first,' says Sid. 'I appreciate that there are some aspects of the business that require attention but you have to remember that for better or worse I represent the management echelon. Golf is the language of management just as Froggy is the language of diplomacy. Why do you think all the Nippons are so dead keen on golf?'

'Because the ball looks much bigger to them?'

'No, Timmo. It's so they can sell lots of transistor radios. They trot round the course talking business and having a swing at the ball occasionally. Incidentally, did you know that washer just fell out of your trouser leg?'

'I don't notice them any more, Sid.'

'Oh well. Please yourself. Where was I? Oh yes — I'd just sliced my first drive into the trees, hadn't I?'

'No, Sid,' I say wearily. 'You were trying to justify learning to play golf while the firm fell apart.'

'Fell apart!' snorts Sid. 'You do exaggerate, Timmo. You're like all those articles in the posh Sundays. Always knocking British management. Well, let me tell you, my lad. We've taught the world a few things in our time.'

'Such as?' I say.

Sid thinks for a few minutes. 'Well, there's golf, for a start,' he says.

'You're being ridiculous, Sid,' I tell him. 'There's no system, there's no planning!'

Sid bashes his hand down on a Dr Barnardo's box which falls apart. 'You can't say that,' he says. 'That's totally unfair. You're dealing with men of foresight and integrity.' He sifts through the change in the Dr Barnardo's box and shakes his head. 'Look at that. Disgusting, isn't it? Three buttons, an old penny and a suspender. There's hardly enough here for a couple of pints.' He looks round the room and pockets the money. 'I'll keep my eyes open for another box,' he says.

'I'll buy you a jemmy for Christmas,' I tell him.

Sid ignores my generosity. 'Where you're so wrong is to imagine that the firm doesn't have a plan. This is totally untrue. Surely you've heard of built-in obsolescence?'

Now Sid comes to mention it, it does ring a bell. 'Refresh my memory, Sid.'

'What is the biggest problem with selling beds, Timmo?'

'Getting them up the stairs?'

'No, Timmo. That's the customer's problem. The big problem is that they last too long. How many times have you heard your mum say, "Oh dear me, Walter. We must get a new bed. This one is falling apart"?. Never, right?'

'That's right, Sid.'

'If you're lucky, you can sell one bed in the course of a lifetime. What we're planning to do is to manufacture beds that fall apart after a few years so the customer has to buy a new one. We have two ways of doing this. First of all we use specially treated materials which have a limited life. Secondly, we have our secret plus — inferior workmanship.'

When Sid rabbits on like this I wonder how I could ever have doubted him. It all makes such good sense, doesn't it?

'In order to make the customer receptive to the idea of buying a new bed we're going to mount an advertising campaign showing a constant stream of new, different and exciting beds. That way, the prospect should get so fed up with his old bed that he'll attack it with an axe before it collapses under him.'

'This is where the professor comes in, I suppose,' I say.

'Exactly, Timmo. We don't expect to sell a lot of the beds he produces. They're just there to create interest and dissatisfaction. We want people to think that new developments are taking place all the time and that you have to change your bed to keep abreast of them.'

I am forced to shake my head in admiration. 'That sounds wonderful, Sid, I wish Umbrage and his lot could have heard you. There's a large body of opinion that thinks of the management as being a bunch of ignorant, parasitic twits.'

Sidney flinches. 'That's so untrue. The board of directors — or the Rightberk family, it comes to the same thing — are a wonderful bunch of people, and they have very low handicaps.'

'You mean, golf handicaps, Sid?'

'No, I mean that only three of them can't read and write. That's much better than the average for the country. I checked with the Institute of Directors.' Sid looks thoughtful. 'Tell you what. It might be a good idea if you came to our next meeting. Then you could pass the word around.'

'Why can't the directors keep in touch with the workers themselves, Sid? I thought you were dead keen on that kind of thing?'

Sid nods. 'I was, Timmo. But I didn't realise how complex it all was. Did you know that Ascot, Wimbledon and Henley come one after the other? You've hardly got time to change your clobber and wipe the strawberries and cream off your mush. And these blokes aren't just directors of one company, you know. Their specialist management skills are at a premium. Their razor-sharp minds are at the beck and call of a number of business consortiums.'

'I never knew that, Sid.'

'Of course you didn't. Neither did I until I got amongst it. It's not all beer and skittles, you know — or champagne and backgammon as we call it in the trade.'

'When is your next meeting?' I say, overcome by a new eagerness to see these giant intellects in full grapple.

Sid produces a small leatherbound booklet trimmed with gold. I note that it has "Director's Appointment Book" engraved on the cover. 'Tomorrow,' he says.

'At the factory?'

'No. At the A.C.D.C.'

'The A.C.D.C.? They're not all bent, are they?'

'Not all of them,' says Sid. 'Blimey. You do get some funny ideas sometimes. A.C.D.C. stands for Artisan Controllers' Dining Club. It's in Berkeley Square.'

'Why do they meet there?'

Sid clenches his teeth irritably before replying. 'It helps to put things in a clearer perspective if you can get away from the scene of immediate involvement. Also there's the question of noise.'

'You mean, the factory is too noisy?'

'No, it's the eerie silence that disturbs some of the

directors. They think better against a background of clinking glasses and rattling knives and forks.'

'It sounds very grand, Sid.'

'It is, Timmo. Don't let me down by eating your peas off the side of your knife. Mash them up with your spuds if you're having problems.'

It is with a feeling of rare excitement that I repair to the A.C.D.C. The more so when I discover that we are eating in a private room — "The De Slurp Room". I get there a bit late because my bus is held up in Knightsbridge and when I enter the room, full of gilt and mirrors, all the seats round the table except one are taken.

I recognise Sid and Rightberk but the other four geezers are unknown to me. They all look like Rightberk in an advanced stage of decay so it is no problem spotting the family resemblance.

'Here at last,' says Sid irritably. 'Gentlemen, this is Timothy Lea. The one what I have been a telling you of.' I can hardly understand his voice it sounds so posh and affected. Maybe he has been having elocution lessons — Dad wanted him to have Electrocution lesson but that is another story.

'The worker chappy, what? I say, let's have a look at him. Jolly droll wheeze. He, he, he!'

'Control yourself, Henry. You've seen a member of the so called working classes before.'

'Have I, Plantagenet? Oh well, if you say so, old bean. Give the champers a fair wind, will you?' The skinny one with the wispy yellow hair drooping over his nut gives another high-pitched giggle and snaps his fingers a couple of times. His neighbour of the surly expression and dewlapped mug continues to glare at me. 'Shoot the lot of them,' he says. 'Total automation, that's the only answer.'

'Come, come, Plantagenet,' says his brother. 'Machines can't raise pheasants, can they?'

'Mother pheasants can,' says Plantagenet.

'Damn me,' says Henry. 'I never thought of that. I always wondered how the heat got to the eggs through those thick serge uniforms Pater used to make the keepers wear. No wonder you were the finest brain of your decade at Oxford, Plantagenet. What say you, Crispin?'

The geezer sitting next to him has his head resting on the table and it does not move.

'Crispin is not feeling himself this morning,' says Jeremy Rightberk.

'That makes a change,' sneers Plantagenet. 'Usually his antics quite put me off my devilled kidneys. Now, what the deuce has happened to those serving wenches?'

So far, I have not been conscious of Slumbernog over-taxing the minds of those sitting round the table but the fifth member of the Rightberk family present touches upon the subject. 'Is that swine Umbrage still alive?' he asks. 'I'd horsewhip him within an inch of his life and then set the hounds on him if I had my way.'

Plantagenet shakes his head. 'Your sensitive nature was always the undoing of you, Maitland. You're as soft as a retriever's mouth to be sure. The only answer with the like of that Trotskyist agitator is instant extermination.'

'God damn it!' says Jeremy. 'You're hopelessly out of touch, you fools. Don't you know that we're living in the nineteenth century?'

'Er — twentieth century,' says Sid.

'Well, twentieth century, then,' says Jeremy. 'Can't be bothered with hair-splitting myself.'

'Don't mind cleaving the odd coney, though, do you, eh, what?' says Henry and they all fall about laughing. All except Crispin who continues to lie with his head on the table. I have no idea what they are talking about most of the time but they do seem a very funny load of blokes. I can understand why Sid isn't saying much.

'The old ways are no longer viable,' says Jeremy. 'You must remember that. Why do you think I've recruited this vulgar little oik to the board?'

'So you can separate him from all his money, I suppose,' says Plantagenet. 'What other reason could there be for having to rub shoulders with such an odious pip squeak?'

It has only just occurred to me that they are talking about Sid.

'The unions,' says Jeremy as if delivering a great truth. 'He talks their language, haven't you noticed? He doesn't sound the ends of his words and he calls supper tea. With him on the board our passage will be eased.'

'My passage will certainly not be eased,' snorts Plantagenet. 'Not by that peasant. Now where — ah, here they are.'

I follow his glance and — by the cringe! — three luscious pieces of frippet are approaching our table with their naked bristols at the full flaunt. Topless waitresses, no less. I never thought I was letting myself in for this when I put on a clean pair of Y-fronts.

'You ordered more champagne, gentlemen?'

'Half an hour ago,' snaps Plantagenet.

'And how would you have it served?'

'Leave the bottles here and go about your business.'

The bird opposite me bends over and her bristols flop on to Crispin's nut like they are trying to hatch it. I have not seen a bigger pair outside those magazines Dad keeps hidden in the hallstand. She bobs a curtsey and then disappears underneath the table. At first I do not think anything of it but when a second bird goes down I wake up to what is happening. Why are they vanishing beneath the voluminous napery? I have not seen anyone drop anything.

'The trouble with this damn country is that there has been a complete collapse of moral values,' says

Plantagenet bitterly. 'Decent human standards just don't prevail any more.' He empties a glass of champagne down his throat and hurls the glass at a distant waiter.

Next to him, Maitland's eyes glaze over and he grips the table with both hands before letting out a low croaking sound. Y-e-e-e-s!' he gasps.

'What do you say, Henry?'

Henry's behaviour is even more strange than Maitland's. He bounces up and down giggling hysterically and eventually plunges his hand into the ice bucket and shoves a handful of ice cubes into his cakehole. While he splutters and squeaks, Crispin slides slowly beneath the table like a ship being launched. It is the first time he has moved since I came into the room.

'Do you think we should call a waiter, Sid?' I say. 'Sid?'

My brother-in-law is slowly rising from his seat and his mouth is opening wider and wider without any sound coming from it. His minces, too, are glazing over as if nipped by frost. I look beyond him to one of the mirrors that line the walls and see a comely arse sticking out from beneath the table. It is moving backwards and forwards like a rounded piston head. What is going on beneath the table? I am about to take a shufti when soft fingers pluck open my fly with practised skill and a tousled female head rises momentarily above table level.

'Sorry to keep you waiting, sir,' it says. 'We're a bit short handed today.'

CHAPTER FIVE

In which Timmy helps deliver a bed to a man-hungry Mrs Collier and hovers on the periphery of an orgy of extravagant sexuality and violence.

When I leave the De Slurp Room it is four o'clock in the afternoon and Plantagenet has called for more champagne and a change of waitresses. I have just disappeared under the table for the third time and I take the chance to crawl away on my hands and knees with the girls. I don't know how they manage to do it and keep their minds fresh for business. The subject has hardly been mentioned so I imagine that they will be discussing the firm's affairs later. There was talk of going on to the Nutcracker Suite for what Maitland described as 'more substantial fare'. I could not keep it up myself — which is certainly something you could not say for Crispin. Though short on words he was a demon when it came to dishing it out at crotch level. Three hours he was at it without stopping. You forgot he was there until his hand appeared above the table groping for another bottle of champagne.

The rest of them didn't seem so keen on straightforward humping. Probably because it interfered with the speed at which they could pour champagne down their throats. I think, too, that the upper classes go a bit more on the kinky stuff. Something to do with strict pot training and greater powers of imagination. Poor old Sid didn't seem to know whether he was coming or going and his posh accent kept slipping every time he made a grab for the table cloth. I think he may have bitten off more than he can chew — which again is not something that can be said about the birds who were performing so valiantly at knee level. As a bunch of nunga nibblers they were in a class by themselves and I will not soon forget the little lady who helped herself to a gobful of ice cubes and gave me my first arctic blow job. Blimey! Talk about 'Tooti Frutti All Rooti!' I was practically shouting 'Mush! Mush!' as she glided over the frozen wastes.

After the A.C.D.C. the factory seems pretty bleak when I roll up at eight the next morning and notice that a sign saying 'Slumbernog' has appeared over the front gate. At least Sid has got something for all the money he must have lashed out. I clock in and trudge over to the cafe where Lenny and Harry are staring into space over their empty tea cups.

'Fancy another one?' I say.

'No thanks, mate.' They both put their hands over their cups as if another drop of cha would be a wicked indulgence. 'Have a nice time yesterday, did you?'

'Very interesting,' I say. I am in a bit of a quandary because I know that Sid wants me to crack up the management as being shit-hot but, in the circumstances, I feel ill-equipped to do so. The only time they mentioned the firm was when saying that Umbrage ought to be shot. It is a point of view, but certainly not one that is likely to get the lads on the shop floor launching an instant increased productivity drive.

'We thought about you when we were having our sandwiches,' says Lenny. 'Didn't we, Harry?'

'That's right. We had a bit of a blitz on it while you were away. I think I've done my back, mind you, but there you go. It's probably no worse than your hernia, is it, Lenny?'

'Give or take a few spasms of excruciating agony, no, Harry.'

'I'm sorry,' I say. 'I hope you didn't overdo it because I wasn't there?'

Lenny shakes his head and then stops and feels his neck. 'No — ooh!'

'One of your spasms?' says Harry sympathetically.

'Just a twinge,' says Lenny. 'It should pass in a few days.'

'I'll make up for it today,' I say. 'I had a blow — er, yes, yesterday, so I'll have a go today. You relax and I'll do it by myself.'

Harry shakes his head carefully. 'Couldn't let you do that. It wouldn't be right. It's not on to let your mates do the work while you skive.'

'But that's what I was doing yesterday,' I say.

Harry looks thoughtfully at Lenny. 'Yes, I suppose you were, really.'

Lenny nods. 'That's right, Harry.'

There is a long pause while Lenny and Harry return to looking into space. Finally, Harry speaks. 'We couldn't do that, though, could we, Lenny?'

Lenny picks up his teacup as if having forgotten that it is empty and then puts it down again. 'No, Harry.'

I am on the point of opening an artery in order to make amends when Umbrage appears at my elbow. 'Have a nice time with your capitalist friends, did you, Nark? I hope you remembered what I said? No betrayal of your fellow workers.'

'The subject hardly arose,' I say.

'Good. Today I want you on Deliveries. Never had any trouble with your Newingtons, have you?'

'Newingtons?'

'Newington Butts: guts. You've never worn a support?'

'No!' I say, not over-thrilled by the thought that anyone could imagine my tempting torso entombed in the kind of article you see when studying the cover of 'The Kiss of The Whip' in the windows of more selective chemist shops.

'Because if you do yourself a mischief and you haven't made a clean breast of your fundaments then the union can't do anything for you.'

'I'm in good shape,' I insist.

'It doesn't matter about the shape. They could win beauty contests and still drop a couple of inches.'

'I'm not worried about my physical condition,' I say, choosing my words carefully.

'Right. Get over to Deliveries when you've finished your tea. You'll probably find that twat Twitterton over there. Don't stand any nonsense from him. He may be Rightberk's nephew but he doesn't amount to a ball of spit.'

'What about us?' says Lenny. 'Are we expected to toil alone?'

'Of course not,' says Umbrage. 'You wait patiently for a replacement and don't do anything rash.'

When I get to Deliveries I find a big bloke smoking a fag end watching two little blokes staggering under the weight of an enormous bed they are trying to push into the back of a furniture van.

'Timothy Lea,' I say. 'Mr Umbrage told me to come here.'

The big bloke nods his head without looking at me. 'Jack,' he says. 'Hang on a minute. We're just loading up.'

Eager to counteract any impression that I am not prepared to pull my weight, I step forward briskly and help the two hard-pressed geezers who are attempting to manipulate the bed into the van.

'HOLD IT!!' The bloke with the fag shouts so loud that the two geezers let go of the bed. It wavers for a moment and then topples over the edge of the loading bay. There is a crash and the noise of splintering wood.

'Now look what you've done,' says Jack.

'I was only trying to help,' I say.

'Help? Do you want to bring the whole place to a standstill? What do you think would have happened if Umby had seen you do that?' I hang my head in shame. 'Out. The whole lot out. You're taking the bread out of those blokes' mouths.'

'But I was told I was on delivering,' I say. 'Mr Umbrage

especially inquired after my fundaments.'

'Delivering, yes. Loading, no. They're two different things, son. Totally different skills involved.'

I look down at the remains of the shattered bed. 'I suppose it would be a stupid question if I asked whether I should pick up the pieces?'

Jack closes his eyes and nods gently. 'Very stupid, Tim. That's the job of the Maintenance Department — or maybe the Cleansing Division. I'm not quite certain. It's gone to arbitration.'

'Either way it would be suicide for us to attempt to move that bed?' I say, allowing a trace of sarcasm to creep into my voice.

'You might as well whip a knife into your guts a couple of times or — if you're in a real hurry — try the toad-in-the-hole in the canteen.'

'So what do we do?' I say.

'Draw another bed out of stock,' says Jack. 'The way Moe and Zack are working at the moment it should take us up to dinner time, nicely.'

I am beginning to think that it is pointless coming to work without a good book, when Twitterton bustles upon the scene. 'What's happening here?' he says. 'Why aren't you — Oh!' He has copped an eyeful of the bed.

'Little accident,' says Jack. 'They don't hold up very well, do they? You wouldn't have to get very fruity on that before you were in trouble, would you?'

Twitterton blushes. 'I'm not interested in that,' he snaps.

'I had wondered,' says Jack.

'The breakage rate amongst our products is quite remarkable,' says Twitterton. 'I've been doing a study of it which I intend to submit to unc — I mean, Mr Rightberk.'

I prick up my ears. Is this the 'Built-in Obsolescence' that Sid was talking about?

'Very distressing,' says Jack. 'Well, if it's all right with you, squire, me and my mate will be getting along to the canteen for a well-earned cuppa. There won't be anything happening here for a few hours.'

'Stay where you are,' says Twitterton coldly. 'A propos of my last remark, I have a job for you. A customer has complained about a bed that was delivered last week and I want you to recover it.'

You need the upholstery department,' says Jack.

'You know what I mean!' hisses Twitterton. 'Bring it back here—'

'But I'm signed up to take out a bed. I'll need completely new documentation to bring one back.'

'48, Woodbridge Gardens,' says Twitterton in a determined voice. 'Mrs Collier.'

'Mrs Collier?' Jack perks up immediately. 'Oh, yeah. Well, you've got to look into complaints, haven't you? I mean, the firm's reputation is at stake, isn't it? We can't have Lumbersnog getting a bad name. Hop in, Tim.'

He is pulling out of the factory gates before Twitterton knows what nearly hit him. I am about to ask Jack what made him change his mind but I don't have to bother.

'Funny business this bed delivering,' he says. 'You wouldn't cocoa some of the things that go on. Women can react in a very strange way when they've helped you struggle round a bend in the stairs with a nine by five. It sort of breaks the ice if you know what I mean.'

'I used to clean windows,' I say.

'Well, you do know what I mean. This Mrs Collier. Phew! I practically had to demonstrate the model before I'd got the legs on it.'

'Has she got a friend?' I ask.

'Any number, I should think. Not many who don't lift the seat, though.'

'She has what you might call an excitable nature, has

she?' I say.

'Like a barrel full of electric eels. Get out of it, you stupid prat!' The last remark is addressed to the driver of a Jaguar he is overtaking. It seems clear to me that Jack is eager to re-establish contact.

48, Woodbridge Gardens nestles in the heart of a square of large terraced houses in Islington. They are all painted in different poufdah colours so that you can tell that they either belong to spades or toffs.

'Here we are,' says Jack, jamming on the anchors. 'Look at them curtains. Show me a set of tastefully draped net curtains and I'll show you a woman thirsty for adventure.'

I had never thought about it before, but, upon reflection, there does seem to be some truth in what he is saying. It is often the very house-proud ones who are the worst — or best, depending upon your way of looking at it. I read somewhere that many women sublimate their sexual desires in housework. If I knew what 'sublimate' meant I would be in a better position to comment, but if it means what I think it means, then I agree.

Jack gives a jaunty rat-a-tat-tat on the door and takes a deep breath. Here we go. Eyes down for the count up. It is quite like old times staring at the polished knocker and wondering what is going to be revealed behind it. The eternal lottery of the bloke who makes a living flogging his wares from door to door. The thrill of the open road. For two pins and a packet of peppermints I would burst into song about it.

'You've come — or is that just my sensation-hungry mind leaping ahead of itself again?'

The bird who is addressing us must only be able to see her navel by looking in a mirror and her knockers lunge forward temptingly like they are trying to jostle their way to the front of a balcony. She has blue eyes, a turned up nose and a mass of golden curls flecked with white which she fidgets with while she is talking. Although it is eleven thirty, she is wearing a frilly housecoat and a pair of fluffy carpet slippers. There is no sign of anything under the housecoat that wasn't attached to her when she was born.

'I've just got out of the bath,' she says, looking straight at me as if answering a question.

'I believe you've had a bit of trouble with the bed,' says Jack, staring down the front of the housecoat like Mrs Collier's knockers are hypnotising him.

'That's something of an understatement,' says the lady. 'Come upstairs.'

Jack and I lock shoulders in the door and start brushing our feet on the front door mat like we want to get rid of the 'WELCOME' sign.

'One of our newer models, wasn't it, modom?' says Jack. 'The Kumfisnuggle Nodoff? We haven't had any other complaints.'

'Perhaps nobody has survived their first encounter with it,' says Mrs Collier. 'It's not supposed to jack-knife every time you get into it, is it?'

'Blimey!' says Jack. 'Perhaps one of the screws has worked loose. That's really a job for our repair service but I don't mind having a look at it for you.'

'I think we may need the repair service as well, says Mrs Collier. 'But come upstairs, darlings. The more the merrier.'

With these encouraging words she swings on her heel and her housecoat swirls in the air to reveal a tempting area of daintily curved back bumper. She must have been sun bathing because you can see the white bit where her panties have been warding off the ultra violet. Once again Jack and I nearly do each other serious injury in the rush for the stairs, and the bannisters quiver.

'Nice place you've got here,' says Jack. He is looking at her arse when he says it but Mrs Collier chooses to interpret the remark as referring to the furnishings.

'Thank you,' she says. 'It's recovered pretty well from your last visit. I suppose I should be grateful that it wasn't a grand piano you were delivering.' As she speaks she fingers a long furrow in the wallpaper and Jack winces.

'I think we should have winched it up and taken it through the bedroom window,' he says. 'Did that cherub's head stick on all right?'

'Excellent,' says Mrs C. 'The only trouble was that you put it on the wrong way round. He should never have been looking into his quiver while he was firing the bow.'

She flings open a door and I find myself looking at Jack's back followed by the interior of a lavishly furnished bedroom. Against one of the walls rests the imposing bulk of the Kumfisnuggle Nodoff.

'Looks all right,' says Jack sounding surprised.

'Don't go away,' says Mrs Collier. 'I want to show you something.' Whilst we stand our ground bravely, she crosses to the bed and performs a graceful backwards flop with arms outstretched. Her gown falls open and we collect a quick flash of fuzz. At the same time, the bedhead falls off.

'That's not right,' says Jack, firmly and positively. He turns to me for confirmation and I nod vigorously.

'Oh good,' says Mrs Collier sweetly. 'It was becoming very disturbing. My husband is not the most passionate and persistent of men and when that thing came down like a guillotine as he was getting into bed, it quite put him off his stroke.'

'I can imagine,' says Jack. 'You'd better go and get the dismantling tool, Tim.'

'You mean the screwdriver?' I say.

'Before your friend goes I'd like to show you both something else,' says Mrs C. She leans back on the bed so that her shoulders are pressed firmly against the counterpane and draws up her legs. The housecoat falls open again and we get the chance to have a gander at her beautifully formed pins — amongst other things. I hear Jack draw in his breath sharply.

'Now, watch this wobble.' So saying, the lovely lady begins to rock backwards and forwards until her housecoat falls open completely and her bristols ripple up and down against her chest like a couple of freshly risen Yorkshire puddings.

'It's incredible.' Jack closes his minces for a second as if testing that they are still on the job.

'Do you see the legs?' says Mrs Collier. She is beginning to puff a bit.

'They're beautiful,' says Jack. His hands are straying to the buckle of his belt and the expression on his face reminds me of the portrait of Sir Richard De Slurp that presides over the room named after him at the A.C.D.C. Club — like a frog about to come.

'I meant the bed's legs,' grits Mrs Collier. 'They don't fit the sockets properly.'

'That's terrible,' says Jack. 'What's it like when you have two people on it?'

'Or three?' I say hurriedly. I mean, the sight of Mrs Collier threshing around like that is very affecting if you are of a suggestible nature and I don't want to find myself having to —

'Go and get the bloody screwdriver,' snarls Jack. He is stepping out of his overalls which suggests that he intends to give the bed a thorough testing.

'But Jack! Don't you think I'd better —'

'Hop it!!' Jack is a big bloke and this does not only apply to what you see when he is dressed up to deliver beds. I see Mrs C. eyeing his space probe longingly. 'I think it needs something with a bigger thread,' she says.

'We'll see what we can do,' says Jack. He turns on me

viciously.

'Go and get me an adjustable spanner. If it's not in the van it will be back at the works — or anywhere.'

I can see that there is not much point in arguing with him so I take a last longing look at the curvaceous Mrs C. and head for the stairs. I bet Jack never shared his toys when he was a kid. I have just got to the bottom of the stairs when there is a tremendous crashing noise and a crack runs along the ceiling of the Collier's lounge. Some pieces of plaster fall into the lamp bowl and the air fills with dust. It sounds as if Jack has found a fault in the legs. I pause for a moment and then a steady thump, thump tells me that my workmate is continuing to probe for faults. After-sales servicing is obviously a strong feature of the Slumbernog promotional effort.

It takes me ten minutes to find an adjustable spanner and when I go back into the house, the hall is full of plaster dust and the lamp bowl is swinging from side to side. I hop up the stairs two at a time wondering if it is time for Timothy to do some testing.

No such luck! The bedroom door is locked and when I look through the keyhole I can only see the soles of Mrs Collier's feet wavering over Jack's shoulders and his big white arse banging up and down like a steam hammer. The room is in a shambles, the bed is now flat on the floor without any legs and folded double. They really have given it a right going over.

'I've got the spanner,' I shout — there is so much noise going on that you have to shout.

I don't hear exactly what Jack says but I think it is something like 'Shove it in a parcel!' It seems a very funny thing to do in the circumstances but when I ask him again, to be on the safe side, he does not say anything. It is hardly surprising really, because he is so deeply involved in what he is doing that he must find any interruption distracting.

Five minutes pass and I have got almost used to the noise when there is a rising crescendo of shrieks and gasps orchestrated by thumps and grunts and capped by a long drawn-out shuddering moan. It occurs to me that orgasm may have been achieved. A few more seconds and the door opens.

'Have you got that bloody spanner?'

'Why? Do you want to tighten up your nuts?'

The bedraggled Jack is not in the mood to acknowledge my attempt at humour. 'We'll have to pass it through the window,' he says.

For a moment, I wonder what he is talking about and then I realise that he must be referring to the bed. 'You've got to the bottom of it, have you?' I say.

Jack looks at me suspiciously. 'Were you watching through the keyhole?' he says. 'That's not a very nice thing to do, you know.'

'Not rushing off, are you, boys?' says Mrs C. slowly drawing her housecoat across her pink titties. 'Won't you stop for a cup of tea or something?'

'That's very kind of you,' I say. 'I wouldn't say —'

'No,' says Jack. 'We'd better get this back to the works. It could be a big job.' He is not kidding. There are springs sticking out of the bed and the striped bit you lie on is all skew-wiff. However, I have enough experience of human nature to know that Jack's desire to scarper is not prompted by a praiseworthy desire to sort out a customer's problem. It is sour grapes. He has shot his lot yet he does not want me dangling my dongler in the same nooky hole.

'Are you sure you've covered everything?' I say. Mrs Collier smiles. She has a lovely smile that woman.

'Everything,' says Jack, striding to the window. 'Look. See that sloping roof down there? We'll ease the bed on to the window sill and when you've gone down below I'll push it on to the roof. You stop it dropping off until I get down to help, then you lift it into the van.'

'It's quite steep that roof,' I say.

'Don't worry. I'll hold it steady until you're in position.'

I try not to watch the way Mrs Collier is massaging Jack's belly with her hands. She obviously can't get enough of it, this woman. At the present rate of progress it does not look as if I can get any of it.

'OK? Come on, then. Give us a hand.'

'I could rustle you up some cocoa in a jiffy,' says Mrs C.

'One, two, three, UP!' says Jack.

'Blimey! It's blooming heavy, isn't it?' I gasp. 'Don't let go till I give you the word.'

'You're so big!' says Mrs C. rubbing herself against Jack like a lovesick moggy. Honestly, I hardly know where to look. I scamper down the stairs and out into the drive. I will have to find something to stand on if I am going to be at chest height to the lean-to roof. I can't see the bedroom window from where I am standing. I get hold of a dustbin and clamber on to it. Above me, the bed rocks up and down on the sill. There is no sign of Jack and Mrs Collier. Don't say they are at it again!

'Yoo hoo!' I trill. 'Ready when you are.'

I am still waiting hopefully when a brand new Triumph Stag convertible appears round the side of the house and crunches to a halt nearly knocking me off my dustbin. A nattily dressed middle-aged bloke leaps out carrying a bunch of flowers. We nod at each other.

'Beautiful, isn't she?' he says.

Mrs Collier has just appeared. Her legs are wrapped round the small of Jack's back and he is carrying her round the room giving her one. I forget that the newcomer can't see either of them.

'Very nice,' I say. I imagine that this new bloke must be one of Mrs C's regulars who pops round for a grind when the mood takes him.

'Three thousand quid on the road,' he says.

'Oh yes,' I say, thinking that however loaded I was I would always have something better to do with the money — and why on the road?

'Goes like a bomb,' says the bloke. 'I've just had her flat out.' Join the club, I think to myself. Blimey! This bird can't get enough, can she? 'What are you doing here?'

'I'm just taking the bed back,' I say.

'Good,' says the bloke. 'My wife got on to you, did she?'

'Not on to me, personally,' I say, watching Jack and the bird continuing to hump each other round the room. 'She —' Wait a minute! 'Wife!' Oh my gawd!

'My wife was very disappointed,' continues Mr Collier. 'When you lay out so much on an article you expect it to give satisfaction.'

'Very understandable,' I say. Out of sight of Mr Collier, his lovely wife is being backed towards the open window. Boum! Boum! Boum! Jack is certainly a champion when it comes to duffing the stuffing out of the furry doughnut. He had better mind out where he is taking Mrs Collier, though. Her pear-shaped posterior has just dealt the bed a mighty thwack. A few more of those and — hey! Watch it!

'I bought this new car to cheer her up a bit,' says Mr C. 'I think I'll just pop in and —'

'Look out!!!'

Jack has just backed Mrs C. on to the window sill and the bed is coming down the roof towards me like it is on the Cresta Run. As I lose my footing and drop into the dustbin, Mr Collier hurls himself to one side and the bed crashes off the roof and smashes through the canvas top of the car. The windscreen is shattered, the bonnet dented, and the chassis buckled. For some reason that I cannot understand the car radio starts playing 'Happy Days Are Here Again'.

Mr Collier covers his face with his hands and looks as if

he is about to burst into tears.

'Oh well,' I say. 'At least nobody was in it.'

CHAPTER SIX

In which Timmy works alongside Professor Nuttibarm in the Development Centre and even more closely alongside the Professor's assistant, Jean, in the Cuddle Chamber — a period of flat-out effort that has an explosive climax.

The next day I am transferred to the New Product Development Department under Professor Nuttibarm. Twitterton does his nut when he finds that we have destroyed another bed and written off a three thousand pound car to boot and actually tries to get Jack and me the sack. This of course is impossible because it comes under the heading of victimisation. When Umbrage hears about it he nearly brings the whole factory out. In fact, Twitterton is dead lucky not to get sacked himself and ends up being severely reprimanded for exceeding his authority.

I feel a bit sorry for Twat-Features — as Twitterton is known to the work force — or Slack Wilt as Plantagenet Rightberk calls it. He is the only member of the staff who seems to care about anything other than number one and he is always running about trying to get things moving. In return, everyone hates his guts. Even his own family don't have any time for him.

'Boy's a damn liability,' I overhear Maitland Rightberk saying one morning when he drops in to borrow brother Jeremy's golf clubs, and receive congratulations for being able to find his way to the factory. 'I always said there was bad blood there. I wouldn't be surprised if some of those stories about his mother and Mad Carew were true.'

'The chap is a disappointment,' agrees Jeremy Rightberk. 'The workers don't have any respect for him. He doesn't behave like a gentleman. Never gets drunk or falls down or tries to rape their women. Always moping around the place whining about productivity. They're not going to follow a chap like that.'

'The deuce they're not!' agrees Maitland, lashing out with his riding crop at a passing worker.

I am very excited about working alongside Professor Nuttibarm, especially after I start reading an article about him in the karsi — I don't mean that the article is about him in the karsi, just that I start reading it when *I* am in the karsi. I am skimming through the pieces of toilet paper that Mum cuts up, looking out for staples, when I see this picture of what appears to be a padded ceiling.

In fact the pads revolve in sections so that they become beds when facing upwards in the room above the ceiling. It is one of the professors many space-saving ideas. Apparently he is much agitated by the population explosion and how we are going to allocate living space to future generations. I am getting quite interested when I find that I have just used the piece of the magazine that continues the article. Since I am prepared to go only so far in my thirst for knowledge I decide that further inquiries will have to be made on the spot.

The Product Development Centre is situated next to the Cuddle Chamber and I wonder how much of what goes on in the latter is personally suprevised by the professor. I suppose that instead of having all those electrodes attached to your body, you find that they have been attached to the bed. A pleasant surprise on entering the building is to find myself cakehole to gob with Jean wearing a white coat.

'What are you doing here?' I ask, registering that an encouraging glint of interest still occupies part of her enormous minces.

'I got a transfer,' she says. 'I thought I might find the work more interesting. You get fed up with stuffing all the time.'

'Very much so,' I say — though that has hardly been my problem of late.

'Are you all right, now?' Jean glances at my feet as if expecting to see a washer roll across the floor.

'Fine,' I say. I don't like to tell her that the last three disappeared when I had the ice cube blow job. It would sound a bit crude coming out with it just like that, wouldn't it? I remember how worried the bird who was blowing my whistle was. She wanted to know where the nuts and bolts were.

'Where is the professor?' I say. 'I'd better tell him I'm here.'

'He's asleep,' she says. 'He spends most of his time asleep — in the winter, sometimes for days at a time. He works in short periods of explosive energy.'

'How fascinating,' I say. 'Unfortunately, I wiped my arse—' I am going to say "on that piece of the article" but I manage to change direction brilliantly '—nal, Hibernian, hibernating! That's what it's called, isn't it? I knew it was something like the name of a football team.'

Jean looks at me warily. 'Er—yes. But it's usually animals that hibernate. The professor is most unusual in his sleeping habits.'

'What are you working on at the moment?' I say. 'I can hardly see a bed in the place.'

'That's what we're working on at the moment,' says Jean. 'Space conservation. Look.'

She walks over to the wall, presses a switch, and a part of the wall drops forward like a drawbridge and becomes a bed.'

'Very nice,' I say. 'But there's nothing particularly new about that, is there?'

'Look.' Jean presses another switch and a second bed swings away from the wall. 'Meet Professor Nuttibarm.'

There, strapped to the bed and sleeping peacefully, is an old man with a long white beard. He is wearing a night-cap and has a separate strap for his beard.

'How long has he been like that?' I ask.

'He started growing the beard last summer.'

'I mean, how long has he been sleeping in that thing?'

'Since he came to work yesterday morning. The professor believes that soon population density will force families to share the same limited accommodation. In order to avoid gross overcrowding, working hours will have to be staggered and one family sleep, whilst the family they share with uses the accommodation for normal purposes. In fact, three families might be able to share the same living unit: one sleeping, one occupying and the other one out at work.'

'I don't fancy that,' I say. 'Supposing you want to go to the toilet in the middle of the night?'

'All the sleeping units are equipped with plumbing. You would merely attach yourself to the appropriate apparatus.'

'Suppose you want to indulge the procreative urge?' I say. At this point I would like to digress for a moment — it's OK, it doesn't stunt your growth. Note the use of posh lingo. I don't say "a bit of the other" or "a spot of in and out". That would be coarse and unrefined. I use an expression that will not offend and that can only impress the bird with my sensitivity and erudicy. I hope you don't mind me pointing out these things but they can make so much difference in one's relationships with the womenkind.

'Yerwhat?' says Jean.

'What happens if you fancy getting your end away?' I say — I mean, when in Rome. You can only bend backwards so far, can't you? When you start bashing your nut on the floor it's time to call a halt.

'Oh.' Jean blushes. 'There may not be any of that. The professor believes that compulsory sterilisation may have to be introduced. Only certain people will be allowed to have urges and see them through to their natural conclusion.'

Makes your hampton run cold, doesn't it? These scientific geezers put the mockers on anything if you give them half a chance. What kind of man can he be, this Professor Nuttibarm, that he dares to pit himself against the forces of nature? As if in answer, there is a long drawn out fart from the bed and the professor opens his eyes. For a second, the beginnings of a smile pluck at the corners of his cakehole and then a worried and disappointed expression settles on his face.

'Donner und Blitzen!' he says. 'I forgot to attach the pipe again. No wonder I imagined that I was swimming in the China Sea. We have to build in a warning light.' He undoes the straps that hold him to the bed and gets out, smoothing his beard and shaking one of his legs.

'It is not easy, Professor,' says Jean.

'You're telling me it is not easy. Last time we fuse all the lights in Battersea, no?'

'Yes,' says Jean. 'Would you like something to eat?'

'No thank you my dear. Just a clean nightshirt.' The professor looks round the room hopefully. 'Any more beds that need a comfort rating?'

'No, Professor. They've all gone over to the Cuddle Chamber.'

'Damn!' says the great man. 'I feel an attack of total torpor coming on. I've been driving myself too hard lately.' He smothers a yawn and sinks into the nearest chair.

'Tell me, Professor,' I say. 'What first interested you in beds?'

'Are you from the national press?' Nuttibarm looks me up and down suspiciously.

'No. I'm Timothy Lea and I've been sent to you as an assistant.'

Nuttibarm nods. 'That's all right then. If you were from the national press it would cost you fifty guineas to ask questions. Now, to answer you I have to begin right at the beginning. When I was born I was very attached to my mother and she was lying on a bed at the time. I think that this might have had a lot to do with it. First impressions are very important, you know.'

'I know,' I say. I remember reading an article about it.

'I remember this period very well,' muses the professor. 'I used to take meals with my mother and always the bed was very much in evidence. I even had my own little bed which, owing to some inbuilt instability factor was not very secure. It would move about a lot and I found this very disturbing. I became determined to secure a firm foundation for myself.'

'So you were off your rocker from an early age?' I say with a light laugh.

The professor does not look as if he finds this as amusing as I hoped he would. 'I don't know what you're talking about,' he says. 'If you have anything you want to tell me, please wait until I ask *you* a question. Now, where was I?'

'You were trying to find a firmer foundation,' I say.

'About this time, I became so preoccupied with the subject of bed that every night I would go and lie down on one for several hours.'

'Remarkable,' I say.

'I was an unusual child,' says Nuttibarm modestly. 'I wasn't interested in splitting atoms and inventing penicillin like other children. I think, in my heart of hearts, that I was still looking for the security that I had lacked when I was a tiny baby. Every time I got on a bed I was waiting for it to start moving.'

'But it didn't,' I say.

'Oh yes it did. One day I got in it with Fritzi Mousepuss,

and boy, did that bed move!'

'So that changed your attitude?'

'You might say that it broadened my terms of reference,' says the professor thoughtfully. 'Sharing that experience helped me to conquer my fear and come to terms with what I call the totality of bed. After that, I was able to get much closer to beds — of course, not having Fritzi Mousepuss underneath me helped too. She was a big girl.'

'Fascinating,' I lie. 'I understand about the beds, but why are you always sounding off about the population explosion?'

'I don't just "sound off" about the population explosion,' says Nuttibarm, smothering a yawn. 'Anything gloomy will do. It's the best way of getting people's attention. If you say anything cheerful, nobody takes any notice of you — or they think you're mad — but if you say that the world is going to end next Pancake Day or that tea drinking causes athlete's foot, then you'll make the top of page three in nearly every paper in the country.'

'Does your work need a lot of publicity?' I say.

'*I* need a lot of publicity,' says Nuttibarm. 'Or rather, I used to. I was a Father Christmas at Harrods, you know. That's where I got the idea for the beard. You can go a long way in life on a long white beard — in fact, I don't think I've ever known anyone with a long white beard who wasn't a success. I wrote to Ted Heath about it but he hasn't done anything.'

'A Father Christmas in Harrods?' I say.

Professor Nuttibarm smothers another yawn. 'I don't know why I'm telling you all this except that you seem a nice, gullible, stupid-looking sort of boy and one has to find some way of filling in the gaps between the sexy bits.'

'I'm very interested,' I say. 'Really I am.'

'Well, it occurred to me one day, while I was sitting there with all these mothers on my lap —'

'Wait a minute,' I say. 'You're supposed to sit the children on your lap.'

'Gott in Himmel!' Nuttibarm smacks his hand against his thigh. 'So that's why they sacked me. I could never understand the reason. None of the mothers ever complained.'

'I expect it was one of the children,' I say. 'Were you giving the mothers the presents as well?'

'What presents?' says Nuttibarm. 'You mean all those toys? I couldn't give them to a grown woman. She'd have thought I was mad. I used to take them home and sell them.'

'Home is in Germany, is it?' I ask.

'No. Crouch End. I sprinkle my speech with a few German expressions in order to make myself sound more authentic. Jean keeps me informed of any old war films on the telly! "Raus, raus, Schweinhunts!" "Ja vole, mein Führer!" "When it's summertime in Heidleburg!!" '

Professor Nuttibarm's attractive tenor voice soars into the roof and I think what a remarkable man he is. There can be few people who have turned a personal interest into a successful career so easily.

'What about qualifications?' I ask.

'The only pieces of paper I believe in are found behind the door marked "GENTS" — if you're lucky,' says Nuttibarm. 'My qualifications are in my head — oh, and I do have a test tube stand I made when I was at school.'

'So you're not really a professor?' I say.

'My first invention,' says Nuttibarm proudly. 'I used to be plain Ron Figgis. It's so easy. You can change your name to anything in this country.'

'What about the Rightberks?' I say. 'Didn't they ask to see your credentials?'

Just let them try!' says the Professor fiercely. 'My water-works are my own affair — which reminds me — Jean, have you found another night shirt yet?' He pats me on the arm. 'It was nice talking to you, lad. But I'm afraid that it's taken a lot out of me. I need to get my head down for a few days otherwise my creative juices dry up.' He looks around the room as Jean appears with what could be a nightshirt over her arm. 'We must have a bed around here somewhere. I don't fancy another bash in that wall till it's dried out a bit.'

'There's the expandable air bed,' she says. 'But that's got a leak in it.' She indicates something that looks like a deflated lilo only bigger — much bigger.

'Marvellous invention, that,' says Nuttibarm proudly. 'Fill it up with air and it sleeps fourteen people — or twenty-two if you all get on well together — yet it stows away in the back of a mini.'

'How do the twenty-two people travel?' I ask.

Nuttibarm spreads his arms. 'Don't expect me to solve all the problems,' he says. 'I'm only one genius.'

'I don't think it's a very big leak,' says Jean. 'If I plugged it in to the air supply it would probably fill up enough for you to sleep on it.'

'Good girl,' says Nuttibarm. 'You do that. I'll slip into my new nightie. It's going to clash with my night-cap but you can't have everything.'

'What do you want us to do?' I say.

Nuttibarm tugs his beard and smiles. 'Why don't you tidy up in the Cuddle Chamber?'

I glance at Jean and she holds my eyes for wicked moment of madness. 'After tea break,' she says.

When we leave Professor Nuttibarm — or Ron Figgis — or whatever you like to call him — he is fast asleep on the air bed. It is still expanding and now covers half the room. I ask if I should disconnect the air supply but Jean says that it is all right.

'It can't go too far with the leak.' Those are the words she uses.

I am feeling quite frisky as we trip across the yard. Jean has nipped away for a few minutes and this is something that birds always do when a spot of nooky is on the cards. Nothing has been said but I feel that this is the moment when our smouldering passion could catch flame. We have two hours until dinner so there is going to be no problem about having to do it in our own time.

'Have you ever been in here before?' I ask as the door creaks open.'

'Not officially,' she says. 'I mean, not in a testing capacity. I came to look once — I mean, there wasn't anyone here.'

She is getting herself in a right old muddle and I nearly have a go at her on the spot. There is a nasty side to my nature that finds flustered ladies a right turn on. I never go a bundle on the ones who have themselves under control all the time. Cool, calm and collected doesn't collect with me.

'What are they testing at the moment?' I ask.

Jean avoids my probing eyes. 'Professor Nuttibarm has designed this batch for maximum comfort when in the dormant position. It now remains to be seen how they will respond to other demands that may be made on them.' To listen to her, you would swear that she was reading it all from a prompt card.

There are four beds in the room, two doubles and two singles. They are all on the bulky side and full of padding as I find when I sit down on one for a moment. 'Squidgy,' I say.

Jean looks the other way as if I have said something very wicked. It occurs to me that she may be a bit on the inexperienced side. Kindly Uncle Timmy will have to take her in hand.

'How does the test work?' I ask.

'There are meters underneath the beds that record the degree of — er stress. After use, the beds are dismantled and their constituent parts examined and subjected to further bench tests.'

'It seems very thorough,' I say, lying on one of the double beds. 'Can you see anything?'

She glances at the front of my jeans and blushes. Percy always gets delusions of grandeur when I lie on my back.

'No,' she says.

'I meant, on the meter,' I say.

'Oh — er, well, no. I wouldn't. You have to do more than just lie on it.'

'How much more?' I stretch out my mit and draw her towards the bed. It is not the kind of dialogue that would have made Noel Coward jealous but, as I have said many times before, it is not what you say, but saying something and knowing when to translate words into actions. If you think back on all the best bangs of your life, I bet you can't remember what you said to each other before you got on the job. Both your minds were on what was going to happen, not what was happening. Once you have started then it is a different matter. You remember the words — at least, I do. I am not so sure about the birds. I think that they can be a lot less sensitive in the sack than some of those books lead you to believe.

'What are you doing?' she says.

'I'm trying to get you on this bed with me. Come on, what have you got to lose?'

I hold my breath while I wait for the answer to this one because I don't fancy pointing Percy west over virgin territory. Despite all the work that has been done, the incidence of virginity in the British Isles has not been completely stamped out.

'I hardly know you,' she says. This is the classic response and nothing to get alarmed about. It can be easily pointed out that sexual intercourse *is* a way of getting to know somebody better — and a very pleasant one to boot.

'I feel I know you,' I say. I deliver this line with great sincerity and my gaze levelled straight into the centre of her minces. This bird has enormous peepers so there is room for error.

'Somebody might come,' she says.

'You never know your luck,' I say.

I tighten my grip on her wrist and yank her on to the bed. Once they have suggested the possibility of interruption you are home and — well, not dry exactly. You have established the course of action to be followed and are working out details. I lean across and kiss her gently on the north and south. She sighs.

'You knew, didn't you?'

'Knew what?'

'That I fancied you.'

'Do you?' I try and sound as if the thought had never occurred to me but is a nice surprise, and wrap it up in another Swiss Miss.

'It's soft, isn't it?' I say. My germans are crawling all over the place so the remark could apply to a lot of things.

'Do you think it's too soft?'

'I don't know. We'd better find out, hadn't we?'

She is not wearing a dress under her white coat and I fold my right hand under the top of her tights and burrow southwards.

'You don't waste any time, do you?' Her hand closes around my wrist but not to push it away. Instead, she plucks at the hairs on my wrist. 'I like men with hairy wrists.'

I kiss her again and indulge in a little hair tweaking of my own.

'You are wicked,' she says. 'I like it when you do that.'

'How about this?' I say.

My digits dive down Rudey Valley and play a couple of piccolo solos. The lady obviously cares for that kind of music because her back arches and she pinches the skin on the back of my hand. I kiss her again and lean across her so that I can feel her bristols ruckling against my chest. The elastic on her tights is beginning to cut into my wrist and that is bad because I have a feeling that I am going to need all the circulation I can muster. If my breath is going to come in short pants, her body had better come out of long ones.

I raise myself on to my shapely knees and guide her tights down towards her ankles making sure that I don't have to dynamite her panites before I set off. The two garments make ideal travelling companions and the journey is uneventful except for a certain amount of resistance from the bed. It really is a bouncy number. If you turned over quickly you would stand a chance of doing it via the ceiling.

Whilst I am clearing the decks for action, Jean is making playful grabs for parts of my body that would not normally be unveiled at the vicar's tea party unless Miss Bracegirdle had put too much sherry in the trifle. My action man kit is never slow to respond to this kind of interest and lunges forward like a coach load of alcoholics hearing the bolt slide back on the pub door. Jean has no sooner broached my breeches than woman's best friend bounds playfully into her eager fingers.

'Oh!' she gasps. 'He is big, isn't he?'

In fact, Percy is dead normal size-wise but he does try awfully hard sometimes and now seems the wrong moment to be modest.

Incidentally, ladies, if you can find the strength to lob out a compliment about your friend's dick, you stand to do yourself a favour in the long run. You don't have to say it's big. Tensile, beautifully marked — anything like that will do. Just as long as you don't say it's sweet — unless you mean taste-wise. "Sweet" is OK for your kid sister's miniature dachshund but it is not going to coax the last ounce of dynamite out of a love-hungry giggle stick.

I am glad that Jean is happy with her new toy and something about the way her fingers are gambolling over the surrounding countryside makes me feel that my fears about her virginal state were groundless. This girl is no stranger to hampton courting. Normally I might proceed to a spot more thread shedding but passions are running high and I reckon that all this foreplay is very overrated. Stick it in and wave it about a bit, that's the best idea. All these books and articles go meandering on about how to arouse birds who just want a good shaft. The poor devils lie there being messed about like a toddler's dinner when they really want to shout "Get on with it!!" Chances are that by the time the bloke has done a chapter's worth, his dick has lost interest and packed it in for the day. Wack it in, not pack it in, that's my motto.

Carrying the principle into action, I kick off my jeans, do a quick back bicycle to get rid of my pants and nuzzle my way in between Jean's accommodating legs. Percy stands poised at the portal and I savour the moments to come. Six inches of throbbing tonk about to sort out God knows how many inches of pulsating pussy. It must be the match of the century, mustn't it?

Jean clearly thinks so. 'Put it in,' she says.

Who could refuse such a request? Percy leaps forward, jerking the rest of my body with him, and disappears into her snatch like a ferret down a rabbit hole. Jean crosses her legs behind my back. What could be better? Well, the bed could be better. The fault I have previously diagnosed is even more pronounced once you start bashing out love's old sweet melody and it is clear that Professor Nuttibarm has not produced a Humpers' Special Mark I. Jean and I bounce up and down like we are having it away on a trampoline and, on one painful occasion, even separate in mid air. I try getting a firm grip of her back bumpers but that puts the mockers on the long piston stroke which is so much a feature of the Lea style. You have got to have the manoeuverability.

'Get on top of me,' I say. This is not one of my best ideas. You know what birds are like — well, I hope you do! They are always slipping off or getting the rhythm wrong and on this bed it is a complete disaster. At the first flick of my hips, Jean sails into the air and damn near puts the kibosh on the whole morning's entertainment. It is fortunate that Percy is a creature of muscle and spirit otherwise he might have needed a splint.

'Ooh dear. Is he all right?' says Jean. 'I'd better kiss him better, hadn't I?'

As it turns out, I don't think anyone could have kissed him better better, if you know what I mean. It is funny how birds change once they are in the sack. I wouldn't have reckoned this chick to be able to suck an ice lolly without blushing but there she is— well, I'd better not say exactly what she is doing. You want to preserve a bit of mystery, don't you?

'Turn over,' I say. I like the kiss of life as much as the next man but you can't be a taker all your life, can you? She scrambles over on to her hands and knees and I bounce up behind her like we are playing shunting. Once again I direct Percy towards the appropriate quarter and she reaches a hand between her legs to make sure that Clapham's Blue Streak is on target. Contact is made and I soar into space.

Jean does not have big knockers but they dangle temptingly like hanging fruit. I squeeze them gently between licked finger tips and unleash a few practice thrusts. Jean makes contented noises and leans forward so that her head rests on her hands. With her in this position I have something to work against and for a few moments of unsullied ecstasy I hear the satisfying "thwack!" of my body against hers. We are still bumping up and down but the situation is under control.

Then I make the mistake of taking my mits off her tits and grabbing hold of the bedhead. I should have learned from my experience — or rather, lack of it — at Mrs Collier's. The moment I really start getting a grip, the bedhead unslots and comes away in my hands. For a moment I hang in space and then — crunch! I dive off the end of the bed and collect a faceful of floor. Thank goodness that Percy is able to demonstrate his elasticity otherwise I might have taken Jean with me or ended up auditioning for the Vienna Boys Choir. As it is, I scramble to my feet and dust my kneecaps — they don't get a lot of credit in these reminiscences but they do a wonderful job of dividing my legs into two parts and I would like to take this opportunity of saying a sincere thank you to both of them — come on, fellows, shuffle out here and genuflect ... Thank you, ladies and gentlemen. Don't applaud too loudly or they'll demand kneeling pads.

I am very upset about falling off the bed. Not so much because of the pain but because of the danger to the romantic mood I have so carefully nurtured. The more sensitive of you will realise that it is difficult to maintain a high level of emotional contact if you keep acting like Charley Drake working piece rate in a custard pie factory.

'Are you all right?' says Jean. I notice that she does not offer to kiss my kneecaps better. It does not break me up because they have never been my favourite erogenous zone — I'm sorry, fellows, I couldn't keep hiding it from you for ever.

'I'm fine,' I say. 'No thanks to your boss. Has he ever heard of nuts and bolts?'

'Oh yes,' she says, very dead pan. 'He's a bit nuts and he bolts every time something goes wrong.'

I always wondered who wrote all those mottos in Christmas crackers. Marvellous, isn't it? Every one is a comedian, these days.

'Let's get on another bed,' I say. I don't wait for an answer but sweep her up in my strong arms and dump her on the next of Nuttibarm's death traps. Luckily, she is light as a feather so it is no problem. In fact, I could run up and down stairs with her all day — which, when you think about it, would be one hell of a waste of a good woman.

There is a look that could be fear, reproach, or wind in her eyes but I am not taking any chances. I must immediately set out to recapture the rapture that was ours. Pulling back my joy stick I soar into the air, bank, and dip my nose sharply into a steep love dive. Kami Kaze Lea they call me.

'Aaaaaaaaaaaaaaaaaaaaaaaargh!!!'

Like Michelangelo painting the ceiling of the Cistern Chapel — always struck me as being a bloody strange name for it, but then these wops are a bit funny like that — I dart a few electrifying colours on to the walls of her spasm chasm. Her back arches like a hump-backed bridge and her digits plunder my barnet like she fancies me doing a Yul Brynner imitation.

'Come on, come on!!' she screeches. When you have been doing this kind of thing as long as I have you soon catch on as to what they are getting at. The lady clearly favours a return match with the old Socket Rocket. Drawing myself up on my faithful knees I enter myself for the lady's open invitation and set off like hell for the winning post.

Surely, nothing can now interfere with the ecstasy that we both so richly deserve? If it was anyone else but me in line for a half share of the ecstasy the answer would surely be no, but what chance have you got with a monicker like Timothy Lea? No sooner have we applied ourselves to each other than the bloody bed starts squeaking like a field full of mice. Professor Nuttibarm must have supplied all the beds in the Cromby Hotel where I used to work (*Confessions from a Hotel*). You only had to sit on one to take your shoes off and the noise drove you spare.

'Oh gawd!' I say.

'Go on, go on!' The lady is obviously going into orbit. In this condition birds don't care about little things like squeaking bed springs. They wouldn't notice if all the walls fell down or if the Black Dyke Mills Brass Band started playing "Oh for the wings of a dove" in their earhole.

This bird doesn't even notice when all the legs fall off the bed. Yes, that's right. All of them. I suppose I should be grateful. One, two, or three would have been more of a problem. At least I am still in the saddle.

'Oh!!! That's fantastic!' She must believe that it was something I did. Her minces are tight closed so there is no reason why she should think any different.

'It's nothing,' I say — believe me, that is what it feels like too: nothing. How much more is Percy supposed to take? I am all for giving a girl a good time but not at the cost of total rupture. There are two more beds in the room and as far as I am concerned they can get somebody else to test them. I believe they still have a few gorillas at London Zoo. Maybe they would like to risk perforating their pectorals.

'Go on, go on!' Jean digs her nails into my bum and jerks her head back.

In this situation there is only one thing to do — give Percy his head — he has already had Jean's and he can't have mine because I'm not double-jointed. Furious that they are denied the opportunity of further disintegration the remains of the bed creak sullenly as I brace myself on my knees — I knew that once I gave them a plug I would never be able to keep them out of the narrative — and drive into Jean like she is the finish of the Monte Carlo Rally Thousands of cheering people line the route, the bunting billows, Plantagenet Rightberk stands in the doorway — wait a minute! I knew this was too good to last.

'Loafing and fornicating!' he snarls. 'Nothing else ever seems to happen in this place.'

'We were testing —' I begin.

'Don't bother to tell me,' snaps Plantagenet. 'You're the pervert with the washers, aren't you?'

'Not any more,' I say.

Plantagenet turns away with a contemptuous wave of his hand. 'Either way, I'm not interested. Where is the chief parasite?'

'You mean Professor Nuttibarm?' I say.

'Correct.' Plantagenet is watching Jean pull on her tights behind a packing case and he taps the ash off his large cigar thoughtfully. Probably a good idea to get him out of here.

'He's working next door,' I say.

'Working? You amaze me.' Plantagenet peels his eyes off Jean like Mum finding a stamp that hasn't been franked and stalks towards the door. 'Come on! Don't just stand there with your shirt tail flapping. Open the door.' Of course, I should tell him to piss off but thousands of years of conditioning as a serf have made it difficult for me not to respond to the orders of my so-called superiors. Obediently, my hand sneaks out for the nob and I practically touch my foreskin as he sweeps through.

'Peasant!' he snaps.

I watch him stalk across the yard, hoping that he will fall flat on his mush, and he turns when he reaches the door of the Development Centre.

'I'm going to put a bomb under you lot!' he shouts.

'Believe me, you're not going to know what hit you!' So saying, he jams his cigar into his cakehole, reaches behind him for the door handle, turns and — BANG!!!

For a fraction of a second I catch a glimpse of a bulging white wall with Plantagenet Rightberk walking into it and then there is an enormous explosion. The blast knocks me back into the cubble chamber, and the two beds we have not tested collapse.

'What was it?' I shake my head as Jean joins me and we creep gingerly to the doorway.

All the windows have been blown out of the Development Centre and there is no sign of Plantagenet.

'Oh no!' Jean claps her hand to her mouth.

'What is it?'

'I must be mad.'

'Why?'

'Somebody did come and mend the leak in the air bed. There was a note about it.'

'Oh no!'

In the centre of the yard, a long white beard flutters to the ground.

CHAPTER SEVEN

In which a pleasant idyll at the Lea home is interrupted by Chief Inspector McGoolygrab and in which Timmy learns some startling news about Professor Nuttibarm and HM Government's interest in beds. Also in which Timmy is tempted — and succumbs.

'Do you fancy some more semolina, dear?'

'No thanks, Mum.'

It is not a difficult decision to make. For a start off, I did not think that they still served up semolina outside schools and prisons. I expect a few lumps, but the way Mum makes it, the lump stretches from one side of the plate to the other. When you bung some jam on to it, it rolls off. Mind you, with Mum's home-made this is not altogether surprising. I thought it was dead simple making jam. You just boiled up some fruit and sugar and poured it into jars. Mum's effort lacks what you might call "body". It is raspberry juice with a few pips floating in it.

Frankly, I think the raspberries she used were a bit far gone. Their fur coats were the only things keeping them together. Mrs Peters picked them for her before she went on her coach tour of the Balkans. That was all very well, but she did not hand them over till she got back — the coach breaking down in Sarojevo didn't help a lot, either. Mum should have thrown them away but she didn't like to, seeing as how they were a gift. It was silly, really, because Mrs Peters would never have known if they went down the karsi or down our throats.

It is while I am trying to scrape some semolina off the underside of the skin that the front door bell rings. Mum goes to answer it and I look at Dad. He looks at me and, as if drawn by magnets, our eyes converge on the waste bin. A quick nod, and we grab our plates and make a rush for it. Dad stamps on the pedal, the lid flies across the room, and I lift the top layer of tins far enough for Dad to start burying the semolina.

'Not so fast!'

The voice makes me jump out of my skin — just like the semolina Dad is tapping into the bin. I whip round to find myself face to face with two blokes in shabby grey macs. One of the faces is faintly familiar.

'Search that bin, Bradshaw.'

'Sir!'

While Dad and I look on, amazed, and Mum appears behind the two blokes, one of them drops to his knees and starts chucking tins out of the waste bin.

'What do you think you're doing?' says Dad.

'What were you hiding?' says the bloke I think I recognise. 'Have you found anything, Bradshaw?'

'It looks like semolina, sir.' The bloke looks around for something to wipe his hands on.

'Semolina!?' Mum pushed forward angrily. 'How did that get there?' Dad puts his empty plate back on the table and wipes his mouth with the back of his hand. Unfortunately, it has some semolina on it which he smears across his mush. 'Were you throwing away my semolina?'

'Anything else in there, Bradshaw?' says the other man impatiently.

'Quite a few tins, Sir.'

'Make a note of them. And take a sample of that-er semolina stuff.'

'Who are you!?' says Dad, wiping the semolina further over his face. 'What do you mean by barging in here? This is a private house. If you're that hungry, the Salvation Army is just down the road.'

'Inspector McGoolygrab,' says the bloke producing a card. He looks at me like I have come in on the sole of his shoe. 'Our paths have crossed before.'

Of course! He was the bloke in charge of the fuzz that searched Beauty Manor after the spot of bother with Wanda Zonker and the Arab geezers. (See *Confessions from a Health Farm* for full disturbing details).

'Oh, Timmy. You haven't got into any trouble, have you?' Mum's distress may be due to the fact that I got myself into a spot of bother when I was a simple unaffected youth. I was conned into helping move some lead off a roof — at the time I thought it was practically slum clearance.

'No, Mum! Of course I haven't,' I bleat.

'I may have to be the best judge of that,' says McGoolygrab, menacingly. 'Search the house, Bradshaw.'

'You haven't been taking beds, have you?' says Mum.

'That's right,' I say. 'I dismantle them and smuggle them out up my trouser leg.' Well, really! You do get a bit fed up with everybody thinking the worst of you, don't you? Especially when it's family.

'If it's about the telly,' says Dad. 'I'm sorry I got a bit behind with the payments. I was a touch choked about not getting the colour, you see. They never explained to me that you had to have a special set.'

I can understand Dad starting to get worried. Half the stuff in the house has been nicked from the lost property office. Mum is already slipping her mits over the teaspoons with BR stamped on them.

'It's nothing to do with the TV set — though we'll check out your licence number. Make a note of that, Bradshaw.'

'That's another thing,' says Dad. 'I don't think they got my postal order. I never got a receipt or anything.'

'Have you got a search warrant?' I say. I used to watch "Z Cars" when I was a kiddy and it was very good for teaching you to speak like a villain.

McGoolygrab dives into the inside pocket of his suit and waves a piece of paper under my hooter. 'Will this do you, smart Alec?' he says.

'Oh the shame of it!' Mum buries her face in her hands and neatly side foots a pair of binoculars under the table as Bradshaw moves to comfort her.

I read aloud from the piece of paper: 'Chief Inspector McGoolygrab. Certain items on your expense account need further clarification. Namely, the sum paid to Miss Fi Fi La—'

'Not that one!!' McGoolygrab dives into his pocket and produces another sheet of paper, headed "Metropolitan Police, Search Warrant".

I nod my head limply. 'It's a fair cop,' I say. 'Which, if I may say so —'

Dad obviously decides that it is time to find a scapegoat, and rounds on me. 'What a blooming marvellous son, you are! You attract trouble like a maggot.'

'You mean "magnet"!' I say. 'Don't you know the difference?'

'There doesn't need to be one where you're concerned,' says Dad.

'That's enough of that,' says McGoolygrab. 'On your way, Bradshaw.'

'What is all this about?' I say. 'I haven't done anything.'

'Would you say that you had been "doing nothing" at what I believe is now called Slumbernog?'

'Now you come to mention it,' I say. 'I haven't been doing much. I think it's probably something to do with —'

'Don't play games with me.' McGoolygrab's eyes narrow into slits. 'What about Double-OH?'

'You mean "OOH"?' I say. 'Who's Ooh?'

'It's a book,' says Dad. 'Blimey. Even I knew that. Tells you who the nobs have been having it off with — on the level, that is.'

McGoolygrab looks from me to Dad and then back to me again. 'You're either very, very stupid or masters of your craft,' he says slowly.

'Thank you,' says Dad. 'It's not often you get a compliment from a copper these days.'

Bradshaw comes in carrying a thick book and looking

excited. 'I think I've found something, Sir,' he says.

McGoolygrab's eyes light up and he snatches the book from his sidekick's hands. 'My God, yes! S dash Z. what is it? Some kind of code book?'

'No, Sir. It's a telephone directory. I meant, inside, sir.'

'Brains aren't everything in this job, Bradshaw. You'd do well to remember that.' McGoolygrab rips open the book viciously and a pile of magazines fall on the floor. Dad immediately tries to pick them up and then checks himself.

'The whole centre of the book has been cut out, sir.'

'I have eyes, Bradshaw.' McGoolygrab must be a right bastard to work for. He picks up one of the books and his eyes widen. 'Never been to Russia, eh?'

'I never said anything about going to Russia,' I say.

'Exactly. That's the point I'm trying to make. You wanted to keep it dark, didn't you?'

'I've never been to Russia!' I say.

'Then how did this come into your hands?' He holds up a book entitled *Dirty Big Girls from Russia.*

'It's not mine,' I say.

Dad looks embarrassed. 'I found it in the street. I thought I'd better pick it up in case a kiddy came across it.'

McGoolygrab shudders. 'It? There's eight magazines here.'

'Well, all of them, then.'

'Then you decided to hide them in order to protect your own family?' says McGoolygrab sarcastically.

'That's right,' says Dad.

'Of course, you could have destroyed them?'

'It's not an easy thing to do in the privacy of your own home,' says Dad. 'I tried flushing one down the karsi and it got stuck.'

McGoolygrab flicks through the magazine and stops short. 'My God,' he says. 'Look at that! That's one of their rocket bases in the Urals, isn't it? I think I can make out the tip of a rocket.'

Bradshaw studies the photograph thoughtfully. 'It's a large photograph of a vagina, sir. What you saw is probably the clitoris.'

McGoolygrab turns the magazine round four times and then nods. 'You could be right, I suppose. Damn Commie swine! They just don't care, do they? Take a look at that couple.'

'Which couple, sir? The one on the right, the one on the left, or the—'

'It is a bit saucy, that one, isn't it?' says Dad, craning over McGoolygrab's shoulder. 'I tell you the one I like. It's—'

'Get off me!' snaps the Chief Inspector. 'The future of the nation is at stake. Bradshaw, collect all the evidence and you, Lea, come with me.'

'Me?' says Dad. 'You can't take me. I'm just an old man enjoying a little innocent filth.'

'Not you. The boy.'

Mum bursts into tears and Dad looks relieved and claps me on the shoulder. 'Don't worry son. We'll stand by you. If there's anything you want, just ask your mother when she comes to visit you.'

And that is that. I am spirited away by the bulls without as much as a how's your father? What makes it worse is that I have no idea about what I am supposed to have done. They keep me hanging around for two hours while they sort out the semolina and all the other stuff they have taken. Then they say they are going to take me to the hospital. You can imagine how I warm to the thought of that. Especially when the police car romps past the Bolingbroke. If they are not taking me to the local saw mill, where are they taking me to?

The place we end up at does not look at all like a

hospital and a lot of nasty possibilities are running through my mind. Are they going to give me the third degree? I don't know what it is but I know it's painful. If I had been aware they were going to shine a strong light in my face I would have brought a pair of shades.

In the vestibule, they are selling the kind of flowers you would only buy if you had to send some to a funeral so I know that it must be a posh place. We go up in the lift with a couple of guys in white coats and the plain clothes dick I am with looks embarrassed as I stare into his eyes. 'How long can we go on meeting like this?' I say. The copper looks the other way and I wink at one of the doctors. 'I think it's the real thing this time,' I say pursing my lips. When we get out of the lift, the copper looks at me as if he wishes he had not left his black jack at home.

Although I am making free with the wisecracks it is only because I am identifying with Humphrey Bogart. If anyone starts hurting me I will be identifying with Timothy Lea. I wouldn't mind the threat of torture if I knew anything — I'd squeal immediately.

'In here,' snaps the fuzz, looking at me as if he could push me through the keyhole. We have made some progress down a corridor and I am facing a door with sixty-nine on it. How nice. I open the door and enter the room. A gaunt man whose mug is vaguely familiar is sitting up in bed.

'Ali,' he says.

'Pleased to meet you, Mr Ali,' I say, thinking that he does not look much like you know who.

'I said "Ah Lea",' he says pronouncing each word like it was causing him pain. 'I wanted to have a few words with you.'

'It's quicker by phone,' I say. 'Cheaper, too, after six o'clock.'

'Always the jokes, eh, Lea?' The bloke leans towards me.

'Don't you recognise me, Lea? Even without the beard.'

'Good heavens!' I say. 'Professor Nuttibarm. I thought you were—' I break off in embarrassment.

'Dead?' prompts the prof.

'Sacked, to tell the truth,' I say. 'How are you? I hear that Mr Plantagenet is well and recuperating in Switzerland for tax reasons.'

'I had a miraculous escape,' says Nuttibarm. 'When Rightberk punctured the inflatable bed I had just awoken to find myself pressed against the rafters.'

'What expansion!' I say.

Nuttibarm looks at the bulge in his bedclothes and smiles. 'Thank you. It seems to keep the wife very happy.'

'I was referring to the rubber bed,' I say.

'Oh yes,' says Nuttibarm, his face becoming serious again. 'Nearly a ghastly tragedy. The loss of one of this country's greatest secrets agents might have been more than it could stand.'

'You mean Plantagenet?!' I say.

'No! Me, you imbecile! At first I thought you might be responsible.'

'Thank you,' I say. 'I think I'm quite responsible, but it's amazing how many—'

'Responsible for the expanding bed exploding!' Nuttibarm wipes his brow. 'That's why I had to have you investigated. I thought someone might have blown my cover.'

'Uum,' I say.

'When that Arab business came up, things looked black.'

'More brown than black,' I say.

'And to think I was going to have you liquidated,' says Nuttibarm wistfully.

'That's serious, isn't it?' I say.

'I used to believe so,' says the prof.

'And then you found out that I was British to the cor blimey and changed your mind.'

'I'm afraid so.'

'Tell me, Professor,' I say. 'Why were you working at Slumbernog?' Nuttibarm looks round the room suspiciously. 'What I'm going to tell you now is absolutely confidential and vital to the continued safety and prosperity of this great country of ours. It must not go outside this room. Is that understood?' I nod. 'I should not be divulging this information but I feel that I owe you some explanation after what happened to your mother's semolina.' I nod again. 'First of all, I am not Professor Nuttibarm.'

'I know,' I say. 'You're Ron Figgis.'

Figgis shakes his head. 'No. I'm— let's just say I'm OOH.'

'Who?' I say.

'Double OH.'

'So that's what McGoolygrab was talking about!' I say. 'It's all becoming clear.'

OOH winces and reaches for a pencil and pad from his bedside table.

'Constable McGoolygrab had better watch his big mouth or he'll be out of the force.'

'Constable?' I say. 'I thought he was a Chief Inspector.'

'He was,' says OOH. 'Now where was I?'

'You were Professor Nuttibarm,' I say. 'Then you were Ron Figgis. After that you—'

'Shut up!' says OOH. 'I was referring to my narrative. Now Lea—' he takes a deep breath '—you didn't seriously believe all that guff about me being a lift boy at Selfridges, did you?'

'I though you were a Father Christmas at Harrods,' I say.

'Oh yes,' says OOH. 'Selfridges was something else, wasn't it?'

I would never describe Selfridges as being "something else", but there you go. It's a question of whatever turns you on, I suppose.

'The point, very briefly, is this. Her Majesty's Government are extremely disturbed by the implications of the population explosion as far as our own already overcrowded islands are concerned. We are totally incapable of supporting ourselves and unless we have the good fortune to be overrun and maintained by our conqueror, the outlook is bleak. What we need is a means of slowing the birth rate down to a trickle. The population of Britain must shrink until a handful of thrifty souls can maintain a self-supporting economy independent of foreign involvement. Do I make myself clear?'

'Absolutely,' I say, wondering what he is on about.

'Now. How to effect this diminution in the birth rate? That is the question. The Government could introduce compulsory sterilisation but this would inevitably lead to abuses and civil unrest. The best thing is to strike at the heart of the problem. The bed. Most babies being born today were conceived in a bed. If we can find some way, or ways, of making bed an infertile area of conception, then we will be on the way to turning the tide."

'Oh yeah,' I say. A nurse has come in and she is a right little cracker. Dead pert and with an arse like a couple of kids' footballs. Even without the black stockings I would fancy her rotten. She fluffs up the flowers and bends over to pick up something the rambling old geezer has dropped. For two pins I would—

'Am I succeeding in holding your attention, Lea?'

'Oh yes, sir.' The nurse goes out and I try and turn up the wick on my interested expression.

'Your encounter with Miss Nippleshow—'

'Nippleshow?' I say.

'*Jean* Nippleshow. That—' OOH chooses his word

carefully '— relationship demonstrated how successful my regime has been.' He searches my face for a response. 'It wasn't just inferior workmanship and sub-standard raw materials, you know. The reason why it was so damnably difficult to achieve the rudiments of a successful mating position on those beds was because I designed them that way!'

'Blimey!' I say understanding why Jean never mentioned her surname. 'So the government employed you to infiltrate the works and put the mockers on nooky. You'd never think they thought about things like that, would you?'

'There are more things in heaven and earth,' says OOH.

'More things than what?' I ask him.

'It doesn't matter.' OOH is beginning to sound weary. I suppose being blown through a skylight by an over-flated expanding bed must take it out of you.

'Thank you very much for telling me all this,' I say. 'Will you be coming back when you're better?'

OOH shakes his head. 'No. I think my own involvement was misdirected by the powers that be. From what I've seen of the Slumbernog operation, from management downwards — or perhaps, upwards in this case — the firm is more than equipped to fulfil all the hopes expressed for it by the British Government without any outside intervention. My only reservation is whether The National Health Service will be able to stand the strain.'

'You mean, from all those dicky beds,' I say. 'Yeah, that is a point.'

I am very heartened by my conversation with this brilliant and important man because it has shown me that whenever there is a big cock-up at national level it was intended. I had always been naive and untrusting enough to think that it was because the nation was run by a bunch of idiots who would be pushed to direct piss into a bucket without someone shouting instructions through a megaphone. I must change my attitude.

'There is only one thing I don't understand,' I say. 'How did you know I was having a spot of in and out with Miss Seethrough—'

'Nippleshow.'

'Nippleshow, if you were being pressed against the ceiling at the time?'

OOH shakes his head admiringly. 'Excellent. I can see that you are not a complete fool — just a gifted trier. I knew you were having a spot of— sexual relations with Miss Titgander—'

'Nippleshow.'

'—Nippleshow because all that took place in the hideously named "Cuddle Chamber" was recorded on film to assist the design department in diagnosing faults and to amuse the directors after board meetings.'

'Blimey!' I say. 'Mr Jeremy isn't going to cocoa the sight of his old lady having it off with Fred Umbrage.'

OOH smiles. 'I have protected him from such a cathartic experience.' "Cathartic", eh? That sounds a bit kinky. I would have thought that Fred Umbrage was a straightforward in and out man, myself. 'I have removed some of the more distressingly overt encounters in order to protect the protagonists and the susceptibilities of the more sensitive viewers. Your own episode is included.'

'That's nice,' I say. 'Could you give us a blow-job — I mean, blow-up!!!' OOH has pulled his bedclothes up to his chin and shrunk back against his pillows. It is so embarrassing. 'Nothing fancy. Just head and shoulders will do. I want one for my mum, see?'

OOH nods his head weakly and reaches out for a glass of water beside his bed. 'Just leave it with me. I'll see what I can do. And now, if you'll excuse me, I'm feeling rather tired.'

As I go out, the nurse comes in and lets down a cinema screen that was hanging behind me. It is all a bit strange, especially the way she and OOH wait for me to go out of the door. By the time I get to the lift I have decided to take another butchers at the situation. You don't often get the chance to see the British Secret Service on the job, do you? I tiptoe back down the corridor and adapt a what-the-butler-saw position at the keyhole, moving the "Do not Disturb" notice to one side. My field of view is limited but I get a good shufti at the bed. OOH is lying on it starkers and the nurse is down to black stockings and starched cap — Cor!! What a turn on! Don't go any further, darling! OOH is watching something — besides the nurse — and I hear the whirr of a projector.

I am afraid that it is all a bit too much for me and, on an impulse, I open the door and go inside. Nursey is just climbing on OOH's chest and he is having to look round her to see the screen which shows Fred Umbrage's bum bouncing up and down between the thighs of an enthusiastic Mrs Rightberk. It is what you might call a situation charged with eroticism.

'Did you leave something?' says OOH, irritably.

'Not yet,' I say, moving towards the bed. 'Move over. I'm staying for the big feature.'

CHAPTER EIGHT

In which the S.C.A.B. trip to Tolpuddle heads for Southend and a good time is had by all — except the parents of the bride and one or two stockbrokers.

'Right,' says Jack. 'Have we got all the light ale aboard?'

'Forty-eight crates.'

'That's the Guinness, isn't it?' says Jack. 'For God's sake, let's make sure we've got enough this year. We don't want to run short again.'

It is the day of The Sedan Chair and Bedmakers Union's pilgrimage to Southend, and Jack is supervising the loading of one of the coaches.

'I don't understand,' I say. 'It's absolutely chocker with booze. Where are the people going to sit?'

'In the other coaches,' says Jack. 'This one is for the spare booze in case we run short.'

'Who pays for it all?' I say. 'The union?'

'Don't be stupid! The management, of course. It's the least they can do to make amends for the cruel wrongs perpendiculared on the brave sons of the soil who were the Tolpuddle Martyrs — Fred will tell you the rest. He got management to cough up. Now, where are you going to sit, lad? It doesn't matter too much on the way out because that's serious drinking and most of the birds are a bit uptight anyway. It's on the way back you want to pick carefully. Stick with me and we'll get amongst those posh tarts from sales. A couple of Babychams and they're anybody's. You can see them looking at you when you go into the office. Wanting you, but frightened to show it unless their mate says, "Eew. Sinking a bit low, aren't we, Doris?"'

'Talking about getting amongst it,' I say. 'How did you get on when you took Mrs Collier's bed back?'

Jack waves his hand up and down in front of his cake

hole. 'I hoped you weren't going to ask me that. There's some things you don't like to talk about, know what I mean? That woman's lust, well, it was almost disgusting some of the things she did to me.'

'Go on,' I say. Percy is all ears.

'No. I couldn't. It might put you off for life. You have to be very sophisticated to even think about some of the things that happened on that billiard table.'

'Billiard table?!'

'Yeah. I must have potted her red more times than you've had hot dinners.'

'Blimey!' While I am marvelling at the wonder of it all, another driver wanders up and tries to help himself to a bottle of pig's ear.

'Piss off!' says Jack. 'That's for the journey.'

'Have a heart, Jack,' says the bloke. 'We'll be off in a moment. Anyway, you owe me a favour for doing that Collier job. Funny woman, wasn't she? In the end I had to give her one to shut her up. Cheers!' He takes a bottle and wanders off. He must be about five-foot-six and has thick pebble glass specs.

'I had a bad cold that day,' says Jack. 'It's never any good when I've got a cold.'

'Yeah,' I say.

'Better chase everybody up.' Jack disappears sharpish and I am left to find a seat.

I am looking forward to the trip because you can't beat a nice day at the briny, can you? A stick of candy floss and a plate of whelks. A stroll along the promenade and a go on the dodgems. Maybe even a dip if the tide is in. When I climb aboard a coach the chars are already singing, "Oh, I do like to be beside the seaside", and one of them makes a grab at my leg as I go past.

'You'll have to watch her, mate!' cackle the others. 'She's a devil when she's had a few.'

I have carefully avoided getting on a coach carrying any of the mattress stuffers and I hope I have not let myself in for anything even more distressing. Being gang-raped by a party of drunken geriatrics does not appeal overmuch.

Everybody around me seems to have a bottle and an acute awareness of how to convey its contents into the cakehole and it is not long before I am being offered swigs or a share of the booze that is being dished out from the back of the bus. I glance at my watch. Half past eight. Not bad going.

'What time will we get there?' I ask my neighbour.

'I don't know,' he says. 'We never got to Tolpuddle.'

'Never got there!?' I echo.

'Fourteen years that I remember setting out through the factory gates and giving three boos for the management and not once can I remember reaching Tolpuddle.'

'What happened?' I say.

My neighbour shrugs and takes another swig from his flask. 'I can't rightly remember,' he says.

How incredible. Still, Dorset is some distance away. We won't have any problems getting to Southend. By the time it is half past nine and we have only reached the City I am beginning to think again. True, the traffic is bad but I did not expect us to stop for someone to be sick and two old ladies to go to the toilet. It isn't easy to find anywhere in that part of London, either. In the end, they have to do it beside the bus. It wouldn't be so bad if we weren't in the middle of London Bridge at the time. The expressions on the faces of those upper crust geezers is really something to see. They turn as pink as the pages of the papers they have tucked neatly under their arms.

'That'll teach you not to get to work on time, you lazy bleeder,' shouts the coach joker to one gent in a bowler hat and somebody leans out of the window and tries to grab his titfer.

'You don't know what work is, you scoundrel!' shouts the City gent turning from pink to scarlet. He tries a spot of fencing with his umbrella and somebody snatches it and chucks it in the Thames. For a moment I think that there is going to be a large scale punch-up. Then, the traffic starts moving and everybody's attention is diverted to getting Mrs Dorrit back on to the bus with her knickers up.

'It's a lovely trip, this one,' says my neighbour contentedly. 'A really lovely trip.' He has finished his hip flask already so I am not surprised that he doesn't remember much about Tolpuddle.

By the time we are heading through Ilford we have collected three bowler hats and a warning from the fuzz for throwing beer cans out of the window. Everybody is in high spirits and the oldsters are singing "Pack up your troubles". My right arm is not exactly going to sleep, either. I have swallowed more booze than usually slides down before closing time on Saturday night.

'Here we are. There's a nice one, Alfie boy.'

'Right-o, Arthur.'

A couple of words with the driver later, we are pulling in to a layby.

'Why are we stopping here?' I ask my neighbour.

'So everybody can stretch their legs,' he says. 'They don't open till half past ten, you know.' I think he is referring to pubs, not legs.

In fact, legs seem to be the last things that get stretched. Throats certainly get stretched as do one or two more private parts of the body, but there is not a lot happening at leg level — unless they stretch under the pressure of the liquid seeping into them. The back of the coach is opened and an impressive array of crates is laid out. After that it is solid boozing with a little light conversation on the side and a lot of light ale going down the tube in the middle. Other Slumbernog coaches pull in beside us and there is a happy exchange of information between the occupants.

'How many thrown up, Jim?'

'Only old Mother Partridge. Once she gets north of the Thames the atmosphere gets too rarified for her. How many with you?'

'Just a couple of the lads. Mixing cocktails, they were, stupid little bastards. I told them: "Never mix brandy with beer".'

'Too right, squire. Diabolical waste. Fair ruins the taste, don't it?'

'Yeah. And it doesn't do much for the brandy, neither.'

Everybody is getting boozed quite happily until somebody looks at his watch and finds that it is twenty-five to eleven.

'Blimey!' says the bloke next to him, knocking back the contents of his glass. 'We'd getter bet a move on. We're schlipping behind sledule.'

I agree with him. I mean, I expected to have finished my first paddle by now. There is not much point in going to the seaside if you arrive just in time to go home, is there?

At eleven fifteen, the coach pulls up outside a pub in Havering and from the rush for the door you would think the bloody thing was alight.

'Lovely,' says the bloke next to me smacking his lips. 'I could just do with a pint.' Anyone would think he had not consumed a hip flask of scotch and God knows how many light ales.

As the day wears on, it becomes clear to me that there are various kinds of drinking. There is light-hearted personal stuff that takes place within the coach, slightly more serious bouts of dousing the tonsils that are enjoyed at the roadside, and honest-to-God boozing which takes place inside pubs. Anything that slips down outside a pub is just killing time. It is not worth considering as far as the real drinker is concerned.

Every time we leave a pub, all the toilets have to be searched to make sure that we have left no one behind and there is a nasty moment in a place called Cranham when we find the karsi door locked and a pair of boots visible underneath it.

'Passed out on the job,' says Jack. 'Right, lads. Who's going over the top?' I manage to avoid copping that detail which is no bad thing, because when one of our lot drops on the other side he finds himself in the company of a local who has fallen asleep over his *Daily Mirror*. That geezer is not too pleased when he wakes up to discover himself sharing the amenities with a complete stranger and a certain amount of unpleasantness ensues. The situation is not improved by our lad saying: 'I'm sorry. I thought you were one of us.'

When he comes out, he has his hand over his eye and he is being chased by a bloke with his trousers round his ankles. As Confucius might have said: 'Bloke with hand over eye run faster than geezer with trousers round ankles.' Our man is out of the door by the time the other bloke has tripped and put his hand in one of the standing urinals whilst trying to keep his balance. I know you shouldn't laugh but it is very difficult sometimes.

By the time we get to Laindon it is half past two and the big question is, should we push on? After a few more pints and some heated discussion, it is closing time and the answer is yes. We will try and reach Basildon.

I know, that's what I thought. What about Southend? Blooming heck! It's only twenty-five flipping miles from London and I brought my bathing costume. But it is no good. The union executive have reached a decision and are going to petition management for a two-day break so that the trip can be made without undue hardship and sacrifice to its members. There is disappointment, of course, but most members take it very well — let's face it, they have been taking it very well all day.

After we leave Laindon the convoy pulls into a layby and it is noticeable that, for the first time, the coach carrying emergency supplies is receiving serious attention. The next few hours are critical ones and Jack is hopping about anxiously. A repeat of last year's fiasco, when apparently the outing ran out of booze, could be disastrous. Fortunately, it looks as if stocks are going to hold out — but only just.

Another thing I notice is that it is now couples who are sneaking off towards whatever cover presents itself rather than individuals with their mugs twisted into expressions of strain. There is nothing like a few gallons of booze to turn a young man's fancy to what birds are thinking about all the time.

I don't know what it is, but somehow the old relentless magnetism doesn't seem to be working so good today. Jean Nippleshow has been as cold as a polar bear's pussy and is now widening her goo goo eyes at a pimply jerk from the sales department — I don't know what he is doing at a union outing wearing a suit. Nobody else seems to want to know. It is doubly choking when everyone else is getting lined up. I don't mind suffering in company but I hate doing it on my tod. I think there has been a sort of unpleasantness — like rape, for instance — when I hear a bird screaming from the bushes. In the end it turns out that she has seen a cow for the first time.

'It was horrible,' she says. 'Horrible. It had things sticking out of it's head and a rubber glove underneath.'

'You want to leave the countryside alone, girl,' says an old stager. 'You don't know what there is out there. Stick in the layby where you're safe. The others nod in agreement and continue to swill down their beer.

When even the birds in the stuffing department give me a wide berth I start to get really worried. There must be something about me that is less enticing than a fish restaurant in the middle of the Sahara Desert. It is not until we are scrambling aboard the buses for the final assault on Basildon that I get an inkling of what it might be. My flies are undone and someone has pinned a notice saying 'Self Service' on my back.

'Don't worry, lad,' says my neighbour, patting me on the shoulder. 'It'll be all right when we get to Basildon.'

But we don't get to Basildon. We are just coasting down the final straight with the old birds in the front singing "I've got a lovely bunch of coconuts", and near pissing themselves at the memories it brings back, when there is an ugly clonking noise and the driver starts cursing.

'Bloody clutch has gone,' he snarls.

'It can't have gone,' says a voice tinged with terror. 'It's five minutes to opening time.'

'You tell that to the bleeding gear box,' says the driver. 'I've got to stop.'

What makes the whole incident even more tragic is that we have run out of beer. Strong men's lips begin to quiver and women cringe.

'There's a place!' screams a bloke. 'Look! The Crudney Arms.'

From the cheer that goes up you would think that Mafeking had been relieved for the second time.

'It's a bit posh,' says someone else. 'They've got a sign saying "No Coaches".'

'I don't care if it's got a sign saying "No Knickers",' says the driver. 'We're stopping!' So saying he steers the coach into the car park and shoves on the anchors.

'Look, Glad. They've got a wedding reception here.'

'Ooh! Lovely!! I do like a nice wedding. I wonder if she's gone off yet?'

When I go down the steps of the coach it occurs to me that I must be plastered. Everything is a couple of shades darker than usual and slightly fuzzy. The building in front of me is all Tudor and black and white stripes but the uprights are wavering a bit more than they ought to be, even allowing for four hundred years. There are a lot of big cars about and some of them are black and white: Black cars, white ribbons. The old girls were right.

'What are you going to do, mate?' says someone to the driver.

'I'll have to ring up a garage. You may have to go home with the others.'

'We'll never see them.'

'Of course we will. We're nearer London. When it's closing time we'll be able to flag them down as they go through.'

'I'm afraid you must have misread the sign. It says, quite distinctly — "No Coaches". Furthermore we are closed until eight o'clock because we have a private wedding reception. I must therefore ask you to be on your way.' The last voice, firm, clipped — and nervous — belongs to a geezer in a gunge-spattered morning suit who has emerged from the hotel at a fast trot, rubbing his hands together.

'Sorry, mate,' says the driver. 'I didn't have no alternative. The clutch has gone on the bugger. I'll have to use your phone.'

'Oh dear. What a disaster,' says the posh geezer glancing over his shoulder nervously. 'It looks so unsightly and the bride will be leaving in a minute. Can't you push it somewhere?'

'Push it somewhere? You must be bleeding joking, mate. It's difficult enough to move the bugger when it's working.'

Morning suit closes his eyes momentarily as the agony of it all drenches his features. 'Major Blackthorn isn't going to like this,' he says. 'You'll have to keep all those people on the coach. I'm afraid they can't possibly—' His voice tails away as the fading notes of "Knees up Mother Brown" indicate that the last of our party are helping each other through the front door of the hotel. 'Oh no!' He starts running towards the hotel.

'Push it somewhere!' repeats the driver. 'I know where I bloody nearly pushed it.'

When we get to the hotel a distinguished looking bloke in wedding clobber is giving our friend a bad time.

'What the devil's going on, Frimble?' he barks. 'Where have all these ghastly people come from?'

One of the chars taps him on the shoulder. 'Do you know where the toilet is, dear? I'm bursting.'

'Haven't you got a drink, mate?' says another of our party? 'You want to get in there. They're giving it away. It's only champagne but it's all right if you're thirsty.'

'Frimble!! I told you to stop serving champagne half an hour ago!'

'I'm most awfully sorry, Major Blackthorn. They're helping themselves.'

This, indeed, appears to be the case. There is a large room leading off the entrance hall and at the far end of it a bar laid out on a long table covered with a white tablecloth. Some of our lads have located crates of champagne beneath the table and having overcome token resistance from a couple of terrified Cypriot waiters are beginning to tear the foil off the bottles.

'Bleeding difficult to open these things, isn't it?' says my old mate, Lenny. 'Oops! Sorry, love.' His apology accompanies a stream of champagne colliding with the earhole of a very toffee-nosed old tart wearing an enormous feathered titfer.

It soon becomes obvious that very few of our party are well versed in the art of opening champagne bottles and the air is filled with whizzing corks and streams of liquid. The upper crust guests huddle together nervously and gingerly accept such offers of refreshment as come their way. It is clear that they have some difficulty in placing the late arrivals.

'But they can't *all* be servants,' I hear one old bag saying.

'They're so familiar,' says another.

'Thank God for some more champagne,' says a bloke knocking back the contents of his glass greedily. 'I don't care who they are.'

Major Blackthorn is doing his nut. 'Don't just stand there, Frimble!' he screeches. 'Send for the police.'

'Don't be stupid, Edgar!' The voice belongs to a huge woman who looks like Willy John McBride in drag. 'We can't have Charlotte's great day ruined by the intrusion of the police. We'd never hear the end of it. We'll have to get her away and deal with these people afterwards.'

'All right, all right!' snaps Blackthorn. 'Have it your way, you always do. But get upstairs and tell her to get a move on. It can't take her that long to change.'

'Fancy joining in the Hokey Cokey, darling? I like big girls.' Before Mrs Blackthorn can indicate whether she would like to accept the invitation of the Slumbernog employee swaying in front of her, there are shouts and screams from above.

'Oh my God! What's happening now?'

There is a rush for the stairs and we get to the landing to find Arthur Dunge, the boilerman, struggling in the grip of two clean-cut young men.

'The filthy swine tried to assault Charlotte!' gasps one of them.

'It's all a misunderstanding,' whines Arthur. 'I'm looking for the karsi, aren't I? I open this door and I see this tart, half naked, with another tart and I think hello, hello, hello! I'm in a knocking shop, aren't I? So I whips out a fiver and I says, Right! I'll take both of you.'

'Disgusting!' breathes Mrs Blackthorn. 'He should be

birched.'

'I want my five quid back,' says Arthur.

'Get your hands off my mate!' says one of the Slumbernog mob.

'Step aside if you know what's good for you!'

Crunch! Biff! Wallop! Like I have said before, I am a bit pissed at the time and I can't really remember who swings the first bunch of fives. All I know is that there is the mother and father of a punch-up and when I come to I am in the back of this Black Maria full of blokes and birds. I have my arms round this fantastic chick wearing a coffee-coloured slip with lacy bits over her knockers and she is dabbing the lump on the side of my nut with a wet hanky.

'You were fantastic,' she says. 'Absolutely fantastic.'

'Thank you,' I murmur. Now she comes to mention it I do recall — I glance across the van and my eyes meet those of Mrs Blackthorn. Her hat has been pulled down over her eyes and she looks even more like Willy John McBride — with a scrum cap on. She looks away from me and leans forward urgently to the bird by my side.

'Charlotte,' she says. 'You've got to pull yourself together. Rodney is very, very upset!'

CHAPTER NINE

In which Timmy shares an unexpected pleasure with his managing director's wife — and is disturbed.

Everybody agrees that it was a very nice Tolpuddle Martyrs Day — everybody that is except Major and Mrs Blackthorn, Rodney, and those of their guests who suffered actual physical damage or worse. Of course, Charlotte goes back to Rodney when we have all been bound over and I expect that they will live happily ever after. It will give them something to talk about in the long winter evenings, anyway.

Back at Slumbernog, life seems a bit humdrum and I am not sorry when excitement arrives in the shapely form of Mrs Jeremy Rightberk. It all starts when I am about to clock off after a spot of overtime. This involved screwing on twenty-four casters and playing five-a-side soccer for an hour and a half — I am not considered good enough for the solo school where sums of up to 15p have been known to change hands in the course of one afternoon.

I am walking past the Cuddle Chamber when I come across Mrs Rightberk bending over the engine of a small Italian motor car — or I do mentally, anyway. In practice I smile pleasantly.

'Do you know anything about these things?' she says.

'Not very much, I'm afraid,' I say, staring at her arse with obvious relish. 'Can't you start it?'

'The engine won't turn over,' she says. 'I thought something might have become disconnected.'

'Shall I have a go?' I say.

'Would you? I'll stay out here and see if anything happens.'

All the time this harmless conversation is going on we are leering and smirking at each other and it occurs to me that this bird is about as ready for a spot of in and out as I am. If that clip of film I saw with OOH and Nurse Waddley was anything to go by she is a right raver. Some of the things she was doing to Umbrage you could be prosecuted for thinking about. I scramble into the driver's seat and fumble for the controls.

'Snug little job,' I say, watching the way her jeans cling to her love box. 'Plenty of poke, too, no doubt?'

'Plenty,' she says, curling out her tongue to touch her upper lip.

Right on! I think to myself. I wonder if the Cuddle Chamber is open? I turn the key in the ignition but the starter just gives a little shudder as if saying 'piss off and leave me alone!'

'You've got a flat battery,' I say, scrambling out without doing any more of my mechanical marvel act. 'Do you want to ring for a taxi or can your husband give you a lift?'

'My husband's playing golf. It had better be the taxi. Is there a telephone round here?' She moves towards the Cuddle Chamber before I have taken a step.

'Probably,' I say, having a quick look round and following her sharpish.

A new batch of beds are waiting to be tested and they look a lot more solid than the ones Jean helped me destroy. Mrs Rightberk runs her finger along one fondly. 'Do you know who I am?' she says.

'Mrs Rightberk,' I say.

'That's right. How clever of you to know. My visits here are even less frequent than those of my husband. You must have seen me with him?'

I shake my head. 'It was someone else actually.'

Mrs Rightberk sighs. 'Poor Jeremy. He takes so much out of himself on the course.'

'On the coarse what?' I ask — I hate being left in suspense.

'On the golf course. He's a slave to those little round

balls.' I nod sympathetically. 'He doesn't have a lot of energy left when he gets home.'

'That's tough,' I say.

'It is. A woman needs to communicate.'

'I know,' I say.

'It can get very lonely sometimes.'

'I'm sorry.'

'You need somebody to fill the gap.'

'Exactly.'

'I think he understands about my needs.' She reaches out and flicks the end of my hooter with her finger. 'This isn't going to find us that telephone, is it?'

'Do you want it to?' I say. This is the kind of handy phrase that means nothing but sounds impressive.

'What do you mean?' She wasn't supposed to ask that.

'I was thinking about your need to communicate,' I say awkwardly.

Mrs Rightberk stretches out a hand again. 'You're a funny boy, what's your name?'

'Timothy Lea, Mrs Rightberk.'

'Call me Rachel.' She slides her arms round me and kisses me on the mouth. 'You can make love to me if you want to. We'll worry about the taxi later.'

'Great,' I say. It is funny, but now that Mrs Rightberk has taken over the initiative I don't feel so Captain Dynamite as I did a few minutes ago. Percy, who was bounding into the ascendant, is now turning the front of my Y-fronts into a hammock.

'Doesn't the idea appeal?' she says, beginning to sound a little cold.

'I'm knocked out,' I say. 'But I-er believe you have to be a bit careful in here. They have hidden cameras or something. It's just like a supermarket.'

'I know all about that. I've seen the end product. Very arousing.' Her hand drops down the front of my jeans and starts a slow movement that would have done credit to Beethoven.

'But don't the management see them?' I say, feeling Percy begin to come alive again.

'Only after I've seen them. I was on very good terms with the professor'.

You, too, I think to myself. They do all right for themselves, these Secret Service blokes. I wonder if you can get an entry form at the Post Office?

'Well, that's all right then,' I say.

I am not just referring to the cameras, either. Down at crotch level my dongler is no longer a dangler and a lot of red corpuscles are beginning to beat their chests and demand action. I slip my arms around Mrs R. and begin to tug up her sweater. I can sense that she is not the type who wants to be read a couple of chapters of *The Wind in The Willows* first. She is wearing one of those stretch bras and I pull it up and fall greedily on the ripe fruit that reveals itself. Mrs R. clearly enjoys the experience because she has led Percy into the light before you can say Roger Carpenter. She tickles my tonk while I nibble her nipples. It is a highly pleasurable division of labours but without any demarcation problems we are free to let our fingers range over wider areas of flesh. I unzip her jeans and we tumble backwards on to one of the beds, tugging and pulling until our threads are in one pile beside the action station.

'Forget about the bed. Test me!' With these challenging words Mrs Rightberk grabs hold of my minge muffler and shoves it into her snatch like a cucumber into a gravy boat. By the cringe! What an experience. I have lain between some powerful thighs in my time but this talented crotch artist could bash the stuffing out of a medicine ball in a couple of minutes. Her mits fold round my bum and she whips up and down so that my goolies feel like a couple of peas spending their holiday in a spin dryer. I don't want to let the side down so I hang on grimly, but it is not easy. I would not have played all that football if I had known the demands that were going to be made on me.

'How do you feel?' inquires my fun-loving companion.

'You should know.' I wince. 'Oooooooh! If you're coming, you'd better hurry up because I'm going.'

With those less than chivalrous words I abandon myself to the mercy of Rachel Rightberk's thighs — and, believe me, they don't know the meaning of the word. Conscious that she has little time to lose, Rachel slams into top gear and roars down the straight, eating up the distance between us until she overtakes me just before the finishing line and disappears through the grandstand in a shower of gaskets.

'That was heaven,' she pants. 'Let's have a little rest and do it again.'

But we don't do it again. We only get as far as the little rest bit — only that turns out to be a long rest. When I next wake up it is to find that Mrs Rightberk and I have dozed off on top of each other and that a very unhappy looking geezer is staring down at us. The expression on his face suggests that he wishes he had a large rock handy and the name on the front of his passport is Jeremy Rightberk.

CHAPTER TEN

In which Slumbernog hovers on the brink of a serious industrial dispute and Comrade Nitya Pullova arrives from the USSR to make a considerable difference.

'It's disgraceful!' shouts Jeremy Rightberk. 'Absolutely disgraceful!!'

'You're right!' says Umbrage. 'I totally agree with you. It is a disgrace.' It is the next morning and I am in Rightberk's office. 'This lad does an extra two hours overtime in the Cuddle Chamber and you refuse to pay him double rate? I'll say that's a disgrace. It's bloody disgusting! Either he gets his money or the whole factory comes out.'

'Listen!!' screams Rightberk turning scarlet. 'Do you seriously think I'm going to stand by while this little swine fucks my wife and gets paid double his normal hourly wage for the privilege!!'

Umbrage looks shocked. 'There's no need for that kind of language. I don't have to stand here and listen to that.' He pauses to allow Rightberk to regain his composure.'You know very well the agreement that was made with the Union concerning Double Time working arrangements. We are loath to see our members exploited but we acknowledge that there are times when the Sabbath must be broken in order to keep in line with the productivity targets laid down by—'

'No!!' screams Rightberk, smashing his fist down on the desk. 'No! No! No! That's got nothing to do with it. I'm not going to pay this creeping parasite a penny for his desecration of the family bed.'

'Family bed?' says Umbrage, leaning forward attentively. 'Is this a fact? Am I to understand that you were testing items not produced in this factory? This puts a wholly different and highly unpleasant complexion on what was up to now a fairly routine matter. I'm going to have to declare your bed black, Mr Rightberk.'

'You can declare it scarlet if you like, you cretin!' snarls Rightberk. 'Haven't you the simple wit to perceive that I'm talking metaphorically?'

At this point, Sid enters, dusting his kneecaps. 'I was just giving Carole—' he breaks off when he sees that Rightberk is not alone 'er-some dictation,' he says.

'I wondered why she'd taken her cushion with her,' says Rightberk unkindly. 'Look. I want your protogé out of this factory toute suite.'

Sid looks blank. 'Wotchasay?' he says.

'Your assistant: out! He's shown no aptitude for anything since he's been here, except—' Rightberk breaks off as if he doesn't like to think about it. 'Anyway. We don't need him. Get rid of him.'

Sid smiles amiably. 'Well, if you really feel like that about it—'

'Wait a minute, wait a minute!' interrupts Umbrage. 'First of all you're trying to swindle him out of his overtime, now you're trying to sack him. This could bring the whole country to a halt. I've warned you once and I'll warn you again: either he gets his just deserts or the whole factory comes out.'

'He is getting his just deserts,' snarls Rightberk. 'He's sacked.'

Umbrage takes a deep breath and places his hands where his braces would be if he was wearing any. 'Very well. On your head be it. I will of course be referring this matter to my executive so that it can be processed through the proper channels, but I can assure you, unequivocally and without fear of contradiction, that I will have the full support of the workers in whatever course of action I choose to recommend.'

'And I can assure you, Umbrage, that I will have the full support of Plantagenet, when he comes out of hospital, and all the other Rightberks — not to mention you, of course, Noggett.'

'Has it come to this, Sidney?' I say. 'Divided across the factory floor. Is this how all your fine hopes and aspirations have ended up? What have you gained by it all, Sid?'

'Well,' says Sid, brightly. 'My golf handicap is down to fourteen.'

'Try and look at it another way, Umbrage,' says Rightberk with an attempt at patience. 'Management in this country can't go on shelling out money forever. The purse isn't bottomless, you know. Supposing I gave this wretched youth his overtime and, as a result of it, the country went bankrupt. What would happen to him then?'

'He'd have more cash to spend on the boat to Australia,' says Umbrage, moving towards the door with an air of finality and a handful of snouts he has palmed while Rightberk was having one of his fits. 'Come on, Lea. Don't worry. The voice of the common working man will be raised on your behalf.'

Rightberk is just observing that working men don't come any commoner than me, when the door opens and Miss Gotcher enters looking flushed. This may be because she finds my presence an embarrassment after the extravagant excesses of our 'Guzzle Fest', as Prudence Packer called it or — more likely — because she has just enjoyed a spot of twat-frotting with Sid. Either way, it has no bearing on the tidings that she brings.

'There's a Miss Nitya Pullova here for Mr Umbrage,' she says.

'Miss?' says Umbrage, taken aback. 'I was expecting a man.'

'I thought you'd been looking a bit plumper, lately,' says Rightberk sarcastically. 'Tell me, pray. Who is this

Miss Pullova and what is she doing here?'

'Comrade Pullova is secretary of the Omsk Branch of the Heavy Metal Workers Union in the workers' paradise of the USSR,' says Umbrage like he is talking about Tom Finney. 'She is here at the invitation of S.C.A.B. as the first part of an exchange visit aimed at creating a greater understanding between the workers of our two countries.'

'God's teeth!' snarls Rightberk. 'As if it wasn't enough having crypto Commies creeping about under the guise of trade unionists. Now we have to have the real thing.'

Umbrage puts on his 'Martyred for the masses' expression. 'I would like to take the liberty of pointing out that the arrangement regarding Comrade Pullova was ratified with the full cognisance of management at a meeting convened on—'

'Oh, shut up!' snaps Rightberk.

'Heavy Metal Workers,' sneers Sid. 'I can just imagine how heavy she's going to be. Putting her weight all over the place and clomping around with her great mounds of flesh wobbling and—'

'Greetings, comrades!'

For a moment, nobody says anything. We stand or sit amazed. Can this beautifully sculpted six foot goddess with burnished tresses and a body like a concrete workers' collective really be secretary of a trade union or are our eyes playing bourgeois revisionist tricks on us?

'Please take a seat, Miss-er Pullova.' Rightberk jumps to his feet so fast that he pulls something. His cakehole opens a couple of inches wider than usual and he makes a grab for the summit of his inside leg measurement.

'Call me comrade, please,' says our shapely visitor sitting down and crossing one gracefully booted leg over the other as she rests her balalaika against a temptingly curved thigh. 'You are Comrade Humpbridge?'

'Umbrage,' says Fred quickly as Nitya addresses herself

to Rightberk. 'Welcome to the squalor that is Slumbernog. I hope that this graveyard of capitalist decadence will not dull your revolutionary fervour.'

'Have no fear, comrade. Yet, I am surprised to find you here. I had believed that we would meet only in the skies.'

'In the Workers' Heaven?' says Umbrage, clearly confused.

'No, but there, too,' says Nitya. 'I had thought that you would take control of my job as I take control of yours. Even now, at Omsk, they are searching the skies for sign of your come.'

'Me coming,' says Umbrage. 'Yes, well-er, I hadn't seen it quite like that. I thought it was more of the cultural visit: twice round the Kremlin, a look at a couple of power stations, and a trip to a vodka distillery.'

Nitya looks unhappy and every man in the room wishes he could do something about it.'Comrade, comrade. I understand your desire to stay here and shatter existing production records but I believe fervently—' she smites her smock between her knockers and her mit almost disappears from sight '— that the cause of international communism can be best served by us spreading ourselves across our brothers and sisters in the movement. Oh my little comrade Humbug! Imagine how it would be at my darling factory at Omsk: at four o'clock in the glorious Soviet morning you awake, light candle and enjoy soul-enriching reading from the immortal works of Karl Marx or some other writer not classified as counter-revolutionary. At five it is time for bran cakes and parsnips, crisp as frostbite. By half past five, your lantern lit and your heart bursting with joy at the thought of the uninterrupted eighteen hours labour to come, you dance down the road to break ice from machines and start work.'

There is a pause while everybody in the room looks at Umbrage.

'Sounds just your cup of tea, Umbrage,' says Rightberk cheerfully.

Umbrage gulps. 'Well-er. Yes, of course, naturally. I think it would be the experience of a lifetime.'

'Six months,' says Nitya. 'Unless you wish to stay longer. Then is matter for discussion.'

'There's no need for discussion,' says Rightberk eagerly. 'I can tell you right now that—'

'I think the point made by Comrade Pullova in her first sentence represents the crux of the matter,' says Umbrage soberly. 'Much as I would like to go, there is so much that remains to be done here. While I'm still granted the strength I feel that I can best serve my brothers S.C.A.B.s by continuing to dedicate myself to their needs.'

'Bravely spoken, comrade,' says Nitya. 'But I am prepared to undertake your responsibilities here while you fill mv hole in Omsk. That was part of arrangement, I think.'

'Yes!' say Sid and Rightberk together.

Umbrage takes another deep breath. 'Comrade. I would counsel caution when listening to the words of these two men. You are not amongst your own kind here. These are capitalists, dedicated to class manipulation and other reactionary bourgeois practices.'

'So,' says Niyta, uncrossing her legs and leaning forward to study Sid and Rightberk closely. 'I have never seen a capitalist before.'

'And I've never seen a Russian bird before,' says Sid leaning forward to deliver the famous Noggett slow burn.'

Umbrage clears his throat. 'At this time, now, the situation is made doubly difficult by the threat of industrial action of quite overwhelming magnitude that is hanging over the company. Even at this moment I am about to convene a meeting of my executive prior to putting a motion to our comrades on the shop floor that they lay down their tools forthwith — if not immediately. At this time it seems to me that it would be an act of cruel and inexcusable selfishness if I, their leader, did not remain here to demonstrate my solidarity with the workers.'

'In other words, there's going to be a strike,' says Rightberk bitterly.

'Strike? What is strike?' Nitya sounded puzzled.

'It's when everybody stops work,' says Sid.

'Stops work?' A note of horror mixes with the amazement in Nitya's voice.

Umbrage steps in hurriedly. 'I think it would be best if I gave you the detailed picture in private comrade. Remember, these men are the enemies of the people. If you would come to my humble office we could—

'Very well,' says Nitya. 'I hope we can also discuss question of where I stay,' She stands up and bows to Sid and Rightberk. 'Good day, comrades. Up the revolution!'

So saying, she sweeps out. I would love to stay and hear what Sid and Rightberk have to say to each other but Umbrage drags me out with him.

In the end, Nitya comes and stays with us. Mum is not over keen on the idea at first because she didn't fancy the end of *Nicholas and Alexandra* but she soon comes round when Nitya gives her a copy of *The Implementation of the Revolutionary Spirit* and a big smile. Nobody seems to be able to resist Nitya. My big worry is when suppertime comes. I know Nitya isn't used to caviar on toast but she must be getting something better than what Mum dishes up.

'Here we are, dear,' says Mum when the evil hour arrives. 'I thought I'd try something special in honour of your visit: spaghetti fish fingers.'

It's amazing, isn't it? You'd think that she would cut up the fish fingers and lose them in the spaghetti if she was going to do anything at all. Instead of that she chops up all the spaghetti and sprinkles it over the fish fingers. 'There's some red currant jelly, if you'd like it,' she adds as an afterthought.

'It's jam, Mum,' I say, but by that time, Nitya has started dolloping it over her plateful.

I watch in horror as she shoves the first mouthful into her cakehole. There is a pause and then, to my amazement, an expression of pleasure illuminates Nitya's face. 'Is good,' she says. 'Very good.' She smiles and squeezes Mum's arm. 'You cook just like my comrade mother.'

When I next see Sid he is smarting with rage. 'That cunning bleeder, Umbrage,' he says. 'You know when he's called the next union meeting? After work! There won't be a bleeding soul there except him and his perishing executive. They'll vote to bring the factory out and the question of him going to Russia won't even be raised.' He clenches his mit and glares at me. 'You know who I blame for all this, don't you?'

'Yes, Sid,' I say. 'Me.'

'Right! if you hadn't got your horrible little private parts enmeshed with Mrs Rightberk we wouldn't be in this mess.' He looks round to see if anyone is within earshot. 'Bit of a goer, isn't she?'

'Have you been there, Sid?' Somehow, Mrs Rightberk seems to get about quicker than Asian Flu.

'Had to, didn't I? You've got to keep in with the right people, Timmo. All these upper class geezers are under the thumbs of their wives. You never know when you might need a word in the right quarter.'

Sid is wrong about nobody turning up to the union meeting. The canteen is packed out. Umbrage takes a step backwards when he sees how many people there are there.

'Greeting, brothers and sisters,' he says. 'I am glad to see that there are so many of you here this evening despite the rival attraction of the European Cup Final between

Slobbo Poko and Groinkic which kicks off on your tellies in ten minutes.' He waits hopefully but nobody moves. 'I can only construe this exceptionally large turnout as indicating how aggrieved you feel about the heinous wrong that has been done brother Lea here.'

'Where's the Russian bird with the big knockers?' shouts a voice from the hall. There is murmur of agreement which shows that the speaker's interest is shared.

Before Umbrage has time to reply, the canteen door opens and Nitya enters. What a sight she is! At first I do not recognise her because she looks so different. Still the same beautiful girl but wearing a dress that I find faintly familiar. Then it comes to me. It is one of sister Rosie's old numbers that Nitya must have found at Scraggs Lane. My sister was never one to conceal her charms and on Nitya the effect is staggering. She is a harvest of curves as she strides down the aisle towards the platform and her nipples stand out like the rivets on the side of a battleship.

'I am sorry that I am so late, comrades,' she says. 'I thought that it would be a good idea to change into local costume for meeting. You like?'

There is a chorus of wolf whistles and Arthur Dunge falls off his bench.

'Er-very fetching, comrade,' says Umbrage. 'I'm certain that Comrade Nitya Pullova needs no introduction from me. You have all seen her about the factory.'

'Not half!!' shouts another voice from the floor.

'Now, let us get on to the nub of the meeting. The serious wrong that has been done Brother Lea. I have enjoyed full and frank discussions with my fellow members of the executive and we have reached the unanimous decision that—'

'Excuse that I interrupt but I know that the words cannot come from your own lips.' Nitya has risen to her feet.

'Thank you, comrade. Your interest is very much appreciated. However it is out of order to interrupt the chair and I must ask you to postpone your comments until such time as—'

'Let her speak!' shouts one of the audience.

'Yeah. Belt up, Fred. We get enough of your rabbit!' complains another voice.

Umbrage looks as if he is going to say something and then extends a hand towards Nitya.

'Thank you, comrade,' says the husky Rusky, brushing her tawny hair from her heart-melting eyes. 'It is for you that I speak. I know that deep down inside you wish passionately to visit Mother Russia yet your praiseworthy sense of loyalty to the cause for which we all fight makes you feel that you must stay here. If you will not listen to me, listen to the voice of your fellow workers.' She turns and faces the audience, her bristols bristling with revolutionary fervour and sequins. 'Will you help me hold the fort so that we can send Comrade Umbrage to Omsk to work shoulder to shoulder with his brothers at the Heavy Metal Works?'

'Yes!!!' roars the audience.

'Wait a minute,' says Umbrage. 'My heart—' But it is no good. Nitya kisses him on both cheeks, and as he slumps into his seat he must reckon that he has already got his plane ticket.

CHAPTER ELEVEN

In which Sid entertains Timmy and pushes the boat out in a big way.

'Nice little wine, this, isn't it?' says Sid. 'Simple without being naive.'

'I'm pissed,' I say. I am, too. It is three weeks after Fred Umbrage left for Omsk and Sid has taken me out to this posh restaurant down by the Thames. He is not usually so generous, certainly not in regard to the booze he has been pouring down my throat. It must all be to do with the way things have been going so well since Fred left. Nitya explained to the workers that strikes were anti-social and that the best way of hitting at the bosses was to exceed the production estimates they had laid down so that management was made to look foolish in the eyes of the party executive. Since she advanced this line of thinking production has gone up five hundred per cent and business is booming.

'Marvellous girl, isn't she?' muses Sid as if reading my mind. 'Every dinner time they group around her while she reads to them from the life of Karl Marx. They've even started putting flowers on his tomb in Highgate Cemetery.'

'I like the way she sings to us with her balalaika,' I say.

'I never knew they had all those Russian versions of western songs; "The Sound Of Mujik", "Where the Boyars are", and of course "Marx, He's Making Eyes At Me".'

'Yeah. That's smashing that one,' agrees Sid. 'Have another drink.'

'I shouldn't really,' I say. But it is too late. Sid has already sloshed the stuff into my glass. 'How are the Rightberks? I haven't seen much of them lately.'

'Well you wouldn't,' says Sid. 'They've gone on a cruise. By the way. Have you ever done any sailing?'

'No, Sid. Why do you ask?'

'Oh, nothing. It's not important. Fancy stretching your legs, do you?'

'I think I'd better,' I say. 'I hardly feel capable of getting to the car.'

Sid takes my arm and steers me out of the door. 'I've got a little present for you,' he says.

'Oh, that's nice, Sid. What is it?'

'It's a jacket, Timmo.' Sid produces this parcel and, I must say, I do get a surprise when I open it. It is all thick material divided up into little pouches. 'Try it on.' I struggle into it and I find it difficult to know what to say. It is very kind of Sid but it is not me, you know what I mean? It even does up with a piece of string at the front and it doesn't have any sleeves. 'How do you like it?'

'Well, Sid,' I say. 'I usually go for something with a bit of a slimmer fit. And yellow isn't a colour I've tried before.'

'You'll find it very handy if you get swept out of bed.'

'Yes, Sid,' I say. 'I expect I — wait a min —'

'Come this way,' says Sid. 'It's nice down here by the Thames isn't it?'

'Yes,' I say. 'Don't walk too fast. I'm feeling a bit woozy.'

'One of the great navigational highways of the world.'

'Yes, Sid.'

'Gateway to excitement and adventure.'

'You could put it like that, I suppose. Is there anyone about? I need a pee.'

'Ever thought about sailing round the world, have you, Timmo?'

'Not for very long. Aaaaaaaah! That's better.'

'Come this way. I want to show you something.'

'Hang on! I haven't bleeding finished yet.' Sid lets go of my arm and I rub my shoe on the back of my trouser leg. 'What is it?'

Sid leads me to the water's edge and points to something

moored to a jetty. 'What do you think of her?'

'It's a bed,' I say. 'A bed floating in the water. It must be that thing that Nuttibarm was messing about with.'

'How would you like to be the first man to sail a bed round the world?' says Sid.

'Are you mad?' I shriek.

'Just think of the prestige for the company,' purrs Sid. 'It would open up markets all over the world. You'd be famous.'

'Famous and dead!' I yelp. 'Here! What do you think you're doing?'

'Just helping you aboard,' says Sid shoving me over the side of the jetty. 'Don't worry. You won't be alone.' He bends down and starts undoing the piece of rope that holds the boat.

'What do you mean? Are you coming?' I wish I could do something but I am so pissed that I have to cling on to the bed to stop my head spinning.

'We'll probably meet up with you in Rio de Janeiro. I thought it was about time Rosie and the kids had a little holiday.'

'Rio de Janeiro?!' I croak.

'That's right. I wouldn't try and do it all in one go. Let the current carry you across the Atlantic and then hop down the coast of South America.' He gives the bed a push and I start drifting out into the river.

'What about food?' I shout.

'There are some tins under the pillow — oh, bugger! I've still got the opener. Catch!' I hear the sound of something plopping into the water. 'Don't forget. Turn right at the mouth of the Thames. Then right again. Then—' His voice fades away into the darkness.

What a carve up! In the circumstances there seems to be only one thing to do: go to bed and hope that things look better in the morning.

THE END

CONFESSIONS FROM A HEALTH FARM

Timothy Lea

At last! Timmy and Sid involved in something healthy. Surely no opportunities here for international intrigue, smutty photographs, and over-taxed bedsprings? All Timmy had to do was spend a week at Bosky Dell Health Farm to see how things were done, then he and Sid would set up their own business.

The trouble was that Timmy wasn't used to living on grapefruit and lettuce, and he certainly hadn't expected to find someone as energetic as Mrs Chalfont next door.

It was a pity Timmy had to leave in such a hurry, but never mind, he'd picked up some good ideas. And with a lady like Wanda Zonker as a partner, he and Sid just couldn't go wrong.

CONFESSIONS FROM THE POP SCENE

Timothy Lea

Teenyboppers, hungry groupies, payola, crooked DJs, foreign tours, golden discs, TV spectaculars, screaming fans and packed out concert halls . . .

For Timmy Lea, always on the lookout for a new career with plenty of openings, Noggo Enterprises spelled success, money and a chance to get his name into the bright lights — providing he could survive the partnership with brother-in-law Sid and his nephew Jason Noggett, the 7-year-old's answer to Mick Jagger, not to speak of Dyke Henna, the transvestite rock star (born Fred Nudger).

Even when business was slow, the manager of Noggo Enterprises found plenty of scope for his talents; in beds, bars and the back seats of sportscars there was always somebody who wanted a little piece of his action.

Would simple, unaffected Timmy survive in the hard world of Pop?

ROSIE DIXON

CONFESSIONS FROM AN ESCORT AGENCY

Nice Girls Don't

The orgy at the Oxford college, the shocking evening at the opera, the disgusting incident in the mini van, the depraved goings-on at the Ugawi Embassy, the unspeakable happenings at Tristram Bingley's photographic studio, the shameless shenanigans at the European soccer match . . .

Is this what working for pint-sized Sammy Fish, boss of Nicetime Escort Agency, is all about? Will Mum's darkest fears be realised, and Rosie's Everest-high principles be compromised? Read the answers to these questions in this stunning sequel to Rosie Dixon's adventures as Night Nurse and Gym Mistress.